D0338846

VERY
WASHINGTON
DC

VERY
WASHINGTON DC

A CELEBRATION OF THE HISTORY AND CULTURE OF
AMERICA'S CAPITAL CITY

WRITTEN & ILLUSTRATED BY

DIANA HOLLINGSWORTH GESSLER

ALGONQUIN BOOKS OF CHAPEL HILL
2009

Published by
Algonquin Books of Chapel Hill
Post Office Box 2225
Chapel Hill, North Carolina 27515-2225

a division of
Workman Publishing
225 Varick Street
New York, New York 10014

Library of Congress Cataloging-in-Publication Data
Gessler, Diana Hollingsworth, [date]
Very Washington DC : a celebration of the history
and culture of America's capital city / written and Illustrated by
Diana Hollingsworth Gessler.—1st ed.
p. cm.
Includes bibliographical references and index.
ISBN-13: 978-1-56512-582-7
1. Washington (D.C.)—Guidebooks.   2. Washington Region—
Guidebooks.   3. Washington (D.C.)—Pictorial works.
4.~Washington Region—Pictorial works.   I. Title.
F192.3.G47 2009
975.3—dc22   2008042445

10   9   8   7   6   5   4   3   2   1
First Edition

**SHIVA NATARAJA
(LORD OF THE DANCE)**
India, state of Tamil Nadu,
Chola dynasty, ca. 990
Bronze
Freer Gallery of Art

In memory of my aunt,
Peg Haldeman,
whom I've always
admired for her
adventurous, curious
nature and incredible
class

1793

the City of Washington

POTOMAK RIVER

EASTERN BRANCH

Part of Virginia within the Territory of Columbia

Part of Maryland within the Territory of Columbia

The original district was 10 miles square, created from land ceded by the states of Maryland and Virginia.

Contents

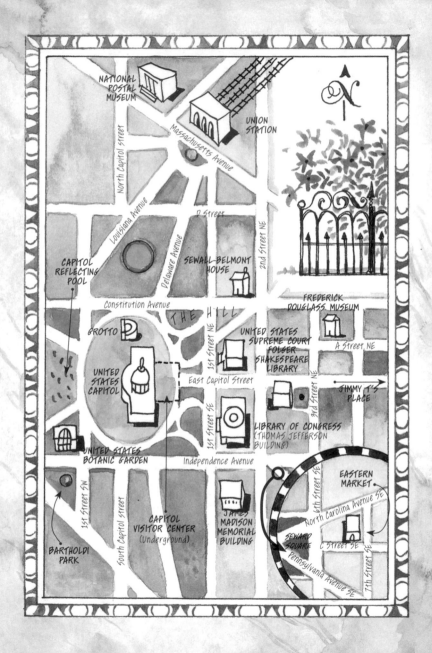

NATIONAL POSTAL MUSEUM

UNION STATION

Massachusetts Avenue

North Capitol Street

Louisiana Avenue

D Street

Delaware Avenue

2nd Street NE

CAPITOL REFLECTING POOL

SEWALL-BELMONT HOUSE

Constitution Avenue

FREDERICK DOUGLASS MUSEUM

THE HILL

GROTTO

1st Street NE

UNITED STATES SUPREME COURT

A Street NE

FOLGER SHAKESPEARE LIBRARY

UNITED STATES CAPITOL

East Capitol Street

3rd Street NE

JIMMY T'S PLACE

1st Street SE

LIBRARY OF CONGRESS (THOMAS JEFFERSON BUILDING)

UNITED STATES BOTANIC GARDEN

Independence Avenue

EASTERN MARKET

North Carolina Avenue SE

4th Street SE

1st Street SW

JAMES MADISON MEMORIAL BUILDING

CAPITOL VISITOR CENTER (Underground)

South Capitol Street

SEWARD SQUARE

C Street SE

7th Street SE

BARTHOLDI PARK

Pennsylvania Avenue SE

CAPITOL VISITOR CENTER
THE UNDERGROUND CENTER FEATURES A TEN-FOOT MODEL OF THE CAPITOL DOME INSIDE AND OUT.

CHAPTER ONE

CAPITOL HILL

Not only was George Washington our first president, but he also selected the location of the new capital, Washington DC, based on his love for the Potomac River.

What is known today as the Hill was referred to as Jenkins Hill by city planner Pierre L'Enfant. It was young America's good fortune that in 1791 L'Enfant had an elegant vision for the new Federal City, as it was then known, and proclaimed the wooded hill "a pedestal awaiting a monument."

But L'Enfant's vision was for future growth and when Charles Dickens visited, he declared it "a city of magnificent intentions," because even by 1842, the broad avenues still led nowhere.

A Journal of my Journey over the Mountains Began Friday the 11th of March 1747/8.

—GEORGE WASHINGTON'S FIRST JOURNAL ENTRY (AGE 16)

GEORGE WASHINGTON KEPT DETAILED JOURNALS ALL HIS LIFE. (Life-size model at Mount Vernon)

George Washington was a sixteen-year-old government surveyor when he fell in love with Virginia's "howling wilderness" and the Potomac River.

As America grew westward, Washington and others believed that the Potomac was the water-way west. He even began a company to develop the trade route via a canal system.

The area around the Potomac—with its George-town and Alexandria ports and midpoint location between north and south—was being considered by Congress for the new capital. After much debate and compromise, it was decided in 1791 that Federal City would be built somewhere along the river's eastern bank.

President Washington was asked by Congress to find the exact site. For several weeks he scouted the river area where he lived, but he had long ago picked a spot—the bowl-shaped area east of Georgetown.

GEORGETOWN

ALEXANDRIA

MOUNT VERNON

GEORGE WASHINGTON THOUGHT THE DISTRICT SHOULD BE SQUARE, BUT THOMAS JEFFERSON THOUGHT IT SHOULD BE A DIAMOND SHAPE.

The Potomac River

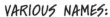

VARIOUS NAMES:

- Co-hon-go-roo-ta (Native American)
- Espiritu Santo (Spanish)
- Elizabeth (first English explorers)
- St. Gregory (Lord Calvert's pilgrims)
- Patawomeck (Algonquin for "trading place")
- Patowmack (George Washington's era)
- Potomac (official spelling 1931)

Painted Turtles

Bass

TO FAIRFAX STONE WV

The drainage area of the Potomac River is about 14,500 square miles.

1608 Captain John Smith is the first European to explore about this far.

GEORGETOWN

WASHINGTON DC

ALEXANDRIA

FORT WASHINGTON

MOUNT VERNON

Ports like Georgetown & Alexandria were regional shipping centers for wheat & tobacco.

"Fish lying so thicke with their heads above water, for want of nets, we attempted to catch them with a frying pan."
—Captain John Smith

Blue Heron

1571 Admiral Pedro Menéndez, founder of Saint Augustine, made the only Spanish voyage & got about this far.

Over 383 river miles from Fairfax Stone to Point Lookout

POINT LOOKOUT MD

Waterlily

The District of Columbia

The District of Columbia is named in honor of Christopher Columbus & is the legal name for the capital, which has had several names:

- Capital City—used by Pierre L'Enfant
- Federal Town—preferred by Thomas Jefferson
- Federal City—named by George Washington
- Washington City—renamed by the first city commissioners to honor George Washington
- Washington DC—another name for the District of Columbia

DISTRICT FLAG BASED ON GEORGE WASHINGTON'S FAMILY COAT OF ARMS

DISTRICT FLOWER AMERICAN BEAUTY ROSE

DISTRICT BIRD WOOD THRUSH

DISTRICT MOTTO JUSTITIA OMNIBUS (JUSTICE FOR ALL), AUGUST 3, 1871

DISTRICT TREE SCARLET OAK *Quercus coccinea*

Pierre-Charles (Peter) L'Enfant
(1754-1825)

L'Enfant was educated as an architect and engineer in Paris before joining America's Continental Army as a volunteer and rising to the rank of major of engineers.

Peter, as he preferred to be called, was passionate about America, so when President Washington asked him to design Federal City, he was ecstatic. His vision was for an open, geometric plan that would grow with the country. When he refused to compromise on any changes to his plan, he was fired with little pay.

"It is not a change in L'Enfant that brings us here. It is we who have changed, who have become able to appreciate his work."

—Secretary of State Elihu Root at the reinterring ceremony of L'Enfant in Arlington Cemetery, 1909

Peter L'Enfant died a pauper and was buried at a friend's home in Maryland. A hundred years later, L'Enfant's plans were finally implemented and he was reinterred at Arlington Cemetery as "Pierre" and a hero.

L'Enfant's Vision

The core of L'Enfant's 1791 design was a triangle of the Capitol, White House, and a monument to President George Washington.

BOUNDARY STONES The Daughters of the American Revolution (DAR) protect the remaining stones that marked the perimeter of Federal City.

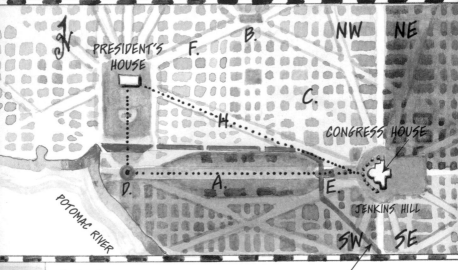

PRESIDENT'S HOUSE

F. B. NW NE

C.

H.

CONGRESS HOUSE

D. A. E.

JENKINS HILL

POTOMAC RIVER

SW SE

L'ENFANT'S ORIGINAL PLAN
(Library of Congress)

CANAL Would flow to the Eastern Branch (Jefferson reinstated its Indian name, Anacostia River)

"Public spaces are outdoor rooms."
— L'ENFANT

A. GRAND AVENUE: Lined with foreign ministries and cultural institutions (National Mall)

B. CIRCLES AND SQUARES: Reserved for monuments of future heroes

C. CITY BLOCKS: Varied in size with the terrain

D. STATUE: President George Washington on horseback (Washington Monument)

E. ARTIFICIAL WATERFALL: Flowing down Jenkins Hill

F. LONG AVENUES: Joined at key points marked by important buildings or monuments

G. TIBER CREEK: Was to be a barge canal (near Constitution Avenue)

H. PENNSYLVANIA AVENUE: Named by Thomas Jefferson

STREETWISE

With the Capitol as the center, the city is divided into quadrants, with street addresses ending in NE, NW, SE, SW.

NUMBERED STREETS
Run north & south

LETTERED STREETS
Run east & west

EXCEPTIONS:
- No J Street. (In early script, the I & J looked alike.)
- Sometimes I Street is written as "Eye Street."
- No X, Y, Z Streets.
- Two B Streets became Independence & Constitution Avenues.

The Capitol 1793

Seven years after George Washington laid the corner-stone, the first building was finished, and over 200 years later, with the addition of the Capitol Visitor Center, "the People's House" is still a work in progress.

CAPITOL'S EAST FRONT

A WOODEN WALKWAY CONNECTED THE TWO ORIGINAL BUILDINGS.

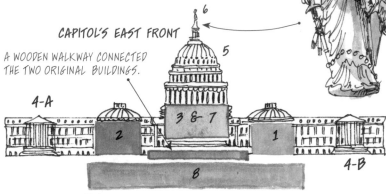

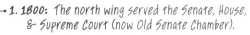

1. **1800:** The north wing served the Senate, House, & Supreme Court (now Old Senate Chamber).

2. **1807:** House of Representatives moved to south wing (now National Statuary Hall).

3. **1826:** Central section connects wings.

4. **1850's:** Grand wings added to the House **(4-A)** and Senate **(4-B)**.

5. **1860's:** Cast-iron dome replaces small copper one.

6. **1863:** "Freedom" statue was cast with slave help.

7. **1958-62:** East front extended to provide dome with better visual foundation.

8. **2008:** Underground Capitol Visitor Center.

Capitol Artists

These are only a few of the artists who devoted their talents to beautifying the Capitol.

WILLIAM THORNTON (1759-1828), amateur architect, won the Capitol design competition. He received $500 & a city lot.

BENJAMIN HENRY LATROBE (1764-1820), British architect, was appointed by Jefferson to oversee work on the Capitol & President's House. His famous corn & tobacco capitals represent early American crops.

CONSTANTINO BRUMIDI (1805-1880), fresco painter, immigrated from Rome & spent his last 27 years creating art for the Capitol. In this dome detail, his wife modeled for "Armed Freedom."

VINNIE REAM (1847-1914) was the first woman & youngest artist to receive a commission from Congress. She was a self-taught, 18-year-old sculptor who wanted to capture Lincoln's "brave, sad face," & when he heard that she was poor, he sat for her.

REAM'S SCULPTURE IS IN THE ROTUNDA.

Frederick Law Olmsted 1822-1903

The founder of American landscape architecture was born in Hartford, Connecticut, and worked as a merchant seaman, journalist, and author before winning the contract to design New York's Central Park in 1857.

When Olmsted was commissioned to redesign the Capitol grounds, he suggested that the building looked too large perched atop such a small hill. So in addition to the landscape, Olmsted designed marble terraces on the Capitol's north, west, and south sides to "gain greatly in the supreme qualities of stability, endurance, and repose."

"I hope you may feel sufficient interest in this rather national object not to have it botched."

—Vermont Senator Justin Morrill granting the commission to Olmsted in 1873

ORNAMENTAL SHELTER BY OLMSTED

The Capitol Grounds
1874

Willow Oak

Frederick Law Olmsted first began work on the east grounds, then the west, north, & south. Almost 300,000 cubic yards of earth were removed to reduce elevation & over 200 trees were transplanted.

PLANTS AND TREES 7,837 were planted, but hundreds were stolen or destroyed by vandals and "trespassing cows."

BRONZE AND GRANITE LAMP PIERS

SUMMER HOUSE OR GROTTO Designed by Olmsted in response to visitors' complaints that there was nowhere to get water for themselves or their horses. Congress denied a duplicate on the south side.

11

United States Supreme Court

Established 1789

A BELL SOUNDS AS THE CLOCK STRIKES THE HOUR & THE JUDGES ENTER THE COURTROOM.

The Supreme Court first convened in the temporary capital, New York City, in 1790 and was presided over by President Washington's appointee Chief Justice John Jay. The Court then moved to Philadelphia and on to the US Capitol before settling into its own building 142 years later.

LISTENING TO ORAL ARGUMENT

The Court hears up to four one-hour arguments a day, three days a week, two weeks a month. Sessions begin in October & visitors may attend oral arguments by forming two lines in front of the building—one for an entire argument, the other for a 3-minute observation.

SCULPTOR JAMES EARLE FRASER CREATED THE INDIAN HEAD OR BUFFALO NICKEL & THE TWO STATUES OUTSIDE THE SUPREME COURT.

CONTEMPLATION OF JUSTICE

12

FOLGER SHAKESPEARE LIBRARY 1932

A lecture by Ralph Waldo Emerson in 1879 at Amherst College sparked Henry C. Folger's lifelong obsession with Shakespeare. By the time Folger retired as president of Standard Oil, he and his wife, Emily, were looking for a place to house their personal Shakespeare collection, the world's largest.

"LORD, WHAT FOOLES THESE MORTALS BE!"

ELIZABETHAN THEATRE
Puck, from *A Midsummer Night's Dream*, welcomes guests to the quaint Folger Theatre.

THE SHAKESPEARE FIRST FOLIO
The Folger has 79 copies of this rare 1623 volume. It is the earliest collection of Shakespeare's works—including *Macbeth*, *The Tempest*, and *As You Like It*, which would otherwise have been lost.

THE FIRST FOLIO IS ON DISPLAY IN THE GREAT HALL WITH PAGES THAT CAN BE TURNED DIGITALLY.

Lavender

"Love-in-idleness"

ELIZABETHAN GARDEN
Planted with herbs mentioned in Shakespeare's plays and plants that were popular in his time.

Library of Congress
1800

The largest library in the world (530 miles of shelves, 135 million items) is actually in three buildings. US copyright law requires that one or two copies of a registered work go to the Library of Congress, meaning about 22,000 items (books, films, music, etc.) arrive at the library daily. About 10,000 are kept; others are put in a Surplus Books Program for distribution.

THE MAIN READING ROOM Visitors to the Jefferson Library view this magnificent sanctuary from a balcony. The library is open to the public with a reader-identification card, obtained at the James Madison Memorial Building nearby.

READER WILL RETURN. DO NOT REMOVE BOOKS.

· 161·

READING ROOM DESK

Getting Around

This Is a TOURist town. There are walking tours, motorized tours, self-guided tours, free tours, river tours, and moonlight tours.

METRO
This user friendly, clean, underground rail service opened in 1976.

TROLLEY & BUS TOURS
Hop-on-hop-off narrated tours

DC CIRCULATOR
Easy-to-use buses service visitor destinations via three routes.

SEGWAY
Glide around town on a self-balancing scooter.

BICYCLE RENTALS

DC DUCKS
Original WWII amphibious vehicles (DUKW) tour the city before diving into the Potomac for a river tour.

RIVER CRUISES
Dining on the Potomac

"The SAGE of ANACOSTIA"

Frederick Douglass (1818-1895) was born into slavery, but learned to read, escaped to freedom, and became one of the most prominent figures in African-American history. With his baritone voice and towering presence he was a powerful, influential lecturer on human rights, the abolition of slavery, and equality for all people.

"I would unite with anybody to do right and with nobody to do wrong." —FREDERICK DOUGLASS

Douglass was a supporter of abolitionist and suffragette Susan B. Anthony, and during the Civil War, he became an advisor to President Lincoln.

"I prayed for twenty years but received no answer until I prayed with my legs." —FREDERICK DOUGLASS

Sewall-Belmont House 1800

FORWARD,
OUT OF DARKNESS,
LEAVE BEHIND
THE NIGHT.
FORWARD
OUT OF ERROR,
FORWARD
INTO LIGHT.

NATIONAL WOMAN'S PARTY 1916

The NWP was formed by Alice Paul & Lucy Burns. They used aggressive tactics borrowed from the British suffrage movement to convince President Woodrow Wilson and Congress to pass the Nineteenth Amendment, finally giving women the right to vote in 1920.

SILENT SENTINELS
PICKETERS WITH
PROTEST BANNERS

ALICE PAUL
(1885–1977)

ALVA BELMONT
(1853–1933)
BENEFACTOR & PRESIDENT

LUCRETIA MOTT
(1793–1880)
ANTISLAVERY & WOMEN'S
RIGHTS ADVOCATE

SUSAN B. ANTHONY
(1820–1906)
ATTEMPTS FOR WOMEN'S
RIGHTS FAILED IN 1878

IN 1929 THE HOME WAS SOLD TO THE NATIONAL WOMAN'S PARTY (NWP) FOR THEIR HEADQUARTERS & MUSEUM.

CLOCK DESIGNED
BY BURNHAM
WITH A ROMAN
NUMERAL IIII
INSTEAD OF IV

Union Station 1907

1870~The Pennsylvania Railroad (PRR) and the Baltimore and Ohio Railroad (B&O) marred the mall area with train depots and tracks.

1901~Each railroad wanted to build larger terminals but bowed to the City Beautiful movement by building a single station in the Swampoodle area.

1907~Union Station opens as the largest train station in the world, positioned by architect Daniel Burnham to face the Capitol as a gateway to the city.

PORTER

1988~Union Station restored in a two-year project.

COFFERED CEILINGS RESTORED WITH
MORE THAN 70 POUNDS OF GOLD LEAF

BENJAMIN FRANKLIN WAS THE FIRST POST-MASTER GENERAL & ON THE FIRST STAMP, 1847.

Colonial America had informal postal routes out of Boston as early as 1639. The British ran its own postal system until the US Postal System was established by the Continental Congress in the late 1700's.

Please feed our chickens, water the cows and the mule in the stable and if the bees have swarmed, put them in a new hive. We have gone visiting.

— Note to a rural mail carrier, 1912

METAL & GLASS MAILBOXES

OWNEY

A stray mutt wandered into the Albany, New York, post office in 1888 & fell asleep on the mailbags. When he began riding with those mailbags on trains across America, railway mail clerks made Owney a mascot & placed tags & medals on his collar for his travels.

Owney's collar became so heavy that the postmaster general gave him a jacket to display his souvenirs. In all, he collected hundreds of medals & even traveled around the world. When he died, mail clerks raised money to have Owney preserved.

ROW HOUSES *A VARIETY OF STYLES SIDE BY SIDE*

"The Hill"

Capitol Hill Historic District was placed on the National Register of Historic Places in 1976 and is one of the largest historic districts in America.

Initially, it was a boarding house community for congressmen who wanted temporary lodging near work.
When the Washington Navy Yard and the
Marine Barracks were established on
the banks of the Anacostia River,
craftsmen also moved into the neighborhood to be near their work, and by 1810
the area was flourishing.

JIMMY T'S PLACE *THIS LOCAL FAVORITE
IS A SMALL DINER IN AN OLD ROW HOUSE.*

20

Eastern Market
1873

L'Enfant's city plan called for public markets, but it was eighty years before Eastern Market became the first in a city-owned market system. It was the unofficial "town center" of Capitol Hill and is the last of the city's original public markets.

BLUEBUCKS

THE MARKET LUNCH
RESTAURANT

FARMERS MARKET

South Hall

THE FLEA MARKET

ARTS & CRAFTS FAIR

United States Botanic Garden 1820

The oldest botanic garden in North America still contains four plants related to the 1842 Wilkes Expedition commissioned by Congress to explore the Southern Ocean.

THE VESSEL FERN, *Angiopteris evecta*, IS A PROGENY OF THE WILKES COLLECTION.

THE GARDEN CONSERVATORY CONSISTS OF 10 GARDEN ROOMS LIKE THE ORCHID HOUSE.

THE NATIONAL GARDEN 2006

Congress authorized the addition of an outdoor national garden funded solely by private contributions. There are various gardens within this three-acre garden.

VOLUNTEER

ADMIRER

The Regional Garden

The Rose Garden

The Hornbeam Allée

BARTHOLDI PARK 1932

The park serves as an inspiration for home gardeners by displaying innovative plant combinations in formal and informal gardens.

GAS LAMPS
FIRST CITY
MONUMENT TO
HAVE LIGHT

PARKING PLACE WITH CLEMATIS VINE & A VIEW

SHELL CLASPS
ON SEA NYMPHS

Bartholdi Fountain

Sculptor Frédéric-Auguste Bartholdi (1834–1904) was working on his design for the Statue of Liberty while creating this fountain for the Centennial Exhibition in Philadelphia. Frederick Law Olmsted, who was designing the Capitol grounds at the same time, suggested that the United States buy the fountain for $6,000.

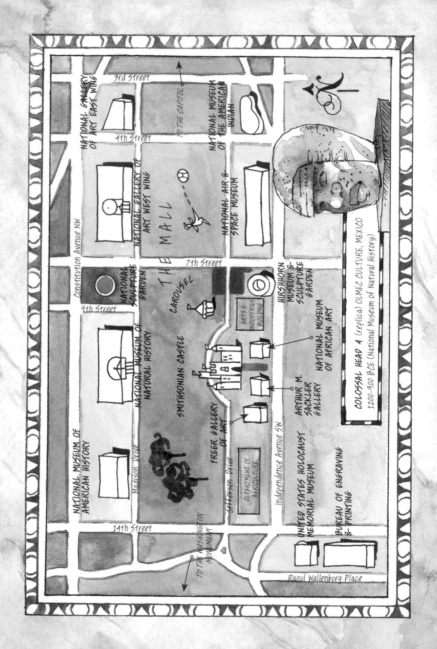

3rd Street

National Gallery of Art East Wing

4th Street

TO THE CAPITOL

National Museum of the American Indian

Constitution Avenue NW

National Gallery of Art West Wing

THE MALL

National Air & Space Museum

7th Street

National Sculpture Garden

9th Street

CAROUSEL

Arts & Industries Building

Hirshhorn Museum & Sculpture Garden

National Museum of Natural History

Smithsonian Castle

National Museum of African Art

Arthur M. Sackler Gallery

National Museum of American History

Freer Gallery of Art

Madison Drive

Jefferson Drive

Independence Avenue SW

Department of Agriculture

United States Holocaust Memorial Museum

Bureau of Engraving & Printing

14th Street

TO THE WASHINGTON MONUMENT

Raoul Wallenburg Place

COLOSSAL HEAD 4 (replica) OLMEC CULTURE, MEXICO
1200–900 BCE (National Museum of Natural History)

"AMERICA'S SMITHSONIAN" IS THE NAME OF THIS PRIVATELY OWNED 1949 CAROUSEL ON THE MALL.

ONE OF 60 CAROUSEL ANIMALS

CHAPTER TWO

MUSEUMS ON THE MALL

The Grand Avenue, as Pierre L'Enfant had envisioned the National Mall, was to be a long, wide park bordered by cultural institutions. But for the next hundred years, his plan was largely forgotten, and the mall grounds were used for grazing cows and buffalo (from a small zoo), a railroad station, and military bivouacking during the Civil War.

In 1902, for the City Beautiful movement, the McMillan Commission restored L'Enfant's plan by creating a long public area with a 300-foot-wide grass carpet bordered on each side by elm trees and great museums. Today, the National Mall extends from the Capitol to the Potomac River.

OVER 2,000 AMERICAN ELMS BORDER THE MALL.

National Museum of the American Indian

2004

George Gustav Heye (1874–1957) of New York began collecting Native American artifacts in 1903. Today more than 800,000 items from the Heye Foundation comprise the museum's core collection.

SEMINOLE DOLL (CA. 1950)

Only twenty-four tribes and native communities are exhibited at a time and rotate out every three to five years. Eight tribes illustrate one of three permanent themes: Our Universes, Our Peoples, and Our Lives.

OUR PEOPLES

Artifacts of Native peoples from North and South America dating to 1491. Sun worship had reached its pinnacle in the Aztec, Maya, and Inca civilizations.

MITSITAM NATIVE FOODS CAFÉ

Mitsitam means "let's eat" in the Piscataway and Delaware languages. There are five regional food stations.

FIDDLEHEAD FERN SALAD FOUND AT THE NORTHWEST COAST FOOD STATION

On the Mall

More than 3,000 free events are held here annually.

SMITHSONIAN KITE FESTIVAL
Kite enthusiasts fly their unique creations.
(March)

SMITHSONIAN FOLKLIFE FESTIVAL
International exposition of living cultural
heritages (June-July)

SCREEN ON THE GREEN
Classic movies shown on a giant movie screen
(July-August)

BLACK FAMILY REUNION
Celebration of African-American family
& culture (September)

NATIONAL BOOK FESTIVAL
Sponsored by the Library of Congress
(September)

WASHINGTON OPERA SIMULCAST
Direct from Kennedy Center, shown on a giant screen
(Various months)

CONCERTS
Memorial Day (May)
A Capitol Fourth (July)
Labor Day (September)
Duke Ellington Jazz (September)

VALET BICYCLE
PARKING BY
NATIONAL PARK
SERVICE

SMITHSONIAN
National Air and Space Museum
1976

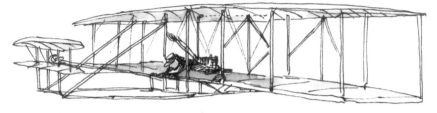

THE WRIGHT 1903 FLYER THE WRIGHT BROTHERS' FIRST POWERED FLIGHT

66 Years Later

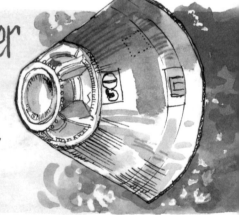

1969 APOLLO 11 COMMAND MODULE, *COLUMBIA*
First manned lunar landing mission, when Neil Armstrong became the first human to walk on the moon

The Smithsonian's aviation collection dates back to 1876 when the Chinese Imperial Commission donated some ancient Chinese kites. In 1946 the Smithsonian's National Air Museum was established but the space race led to a name change and new building on the Mall in 1976. However, only about 10% of the collection was able to be exhibited there, prompting the building of a second facility near Dulles Airport, the Steven F. Udvar-Hazy Center, in 2003.

SMITHSONIAN
Hirshhorn Museum and Sculpture Garden 1974

Joseph H. Hirshhorn (1899-1981) was just six when he arrived in New York from Latvia with his widowed mother and 13 siblings. He left school at 13 to work on Wall Street and bought his first art piece at 18. Later his successful investment in uranium mines allowed him to become a well-known collector of modern art and sculpture.

Juan Muñoz
Last Conversation Piece
1994-1995

ARCHITECT GORDON BUNSHAFT CONCEIVED THE HIRSHHORN BUILDING AS "A LARGE PIECE OF FUNCTIONAL SCULPTURE."

A PANORAMIC VIEW OF THE MALL

Giacomo Manzù
Young Girl on a Chair
1955

Smithsonian Castle
1855

The Smithsonian Institution Building housed all aspects of the institution until 1910. Today it is the Smithsonian Information Center with an orientation video, café, and exhibits from all the institution's museums.

Congress asked James Renwick Jr. to design "a suitable building of plain and durable materials. . . without unnecessary ornament."

A CORNER OF THE ENID A. HAUPT GARDEN PARTERRE IN THE SMITHSONIAN SOUTH YARD

JAMES SMITHSON (1765-1829), a British scientist, never saw America, so it's curious why he bequeathed $508,318 (equivalent to $10 million today) and a mineral collection to a country he never visited. Yet his will stated that if his nephew should die without heirs (he did), the estate should go to Washington DC to build "an establishment for the increase and diffusion of knowledge among men" and be named the Smithsonian Institution.

Alexander Graham Bell, a regent of the Smithsonian, brought Smithson's remains here from Italy. The sarcophagus right inside the door says he was 75 when he died, but he was 64.

Smithsonian Museums

ON THE MALL
Arthur M. Sackler Gallery
Arts and Industries Building (Closed)
Freer Gallery of Art
Hirshhorn Museum and Sculpture Garden
National Air and Space Museum
The National Gallery of Art (Affiliated)
National Museum of African Art
National Museum of American History
National Museum of the American Indian
National Museum of Natural History
Smithsonian Institution Building

BOBBY ORR'S
HOCKEY SKATES

LIVE PANDA CAM

AROUND TOWN
Anacostia Community Museum
National Portrait Gallery
National Postal Museum
National Zoological Park
Renwick Gallery
Smithsonian American Art Museum

OUT OF TOWN
Cooper-Hewitt, National Design Museum, New York City
National Air and Space Museum's Steven F. Udvar-Hazy Center,
Chantilly VA
National Museum of the American Indian's
George Gustav Heye Center, New York City

Many other museums are Smithsonian affiliates.

Freer Gallery of Art 1923

The Smithsonian's first art museum was funded by Charles Lang Freer (1854–1919) to display his biblical manuscripts, Asian art, and the works of a few American artists, like James Whistler. In fact, it was Whistler who encouraged his patron, Charles Freer, to get more involved in Asian art.

THE FOUR GOSPELS (CODEX WASHINGTONENSIS) The third-oldest of the 3,000 known Gospel manuscripts (Freer Gallery owns six) from the 3rd to 6th centuries.

MANUSCRIPT IS BOUND BY PAINTED WOOD COVERS (Detail)

"HARMONY IN BLUE AND GOLD: THE PEACOCK ROOM"

James McNeill Whistler (1834–1903) was asked by Frederick Leyland to add a few touches to his new London dining room, which displayed a porcelain collection and Whistler's painting *The Princess from the Land of Porcelain.* Unbeknownst to Leyland, Whistler became inspired and painted peacocks all over the room. When Leyland refused to pay him, the artist spitefully painted every inch of the room, including the shutters and expensive leather ceiling.

THIS COMPLETE ROOM, PURCHASED BY FREER, UNITES HIS COLLECTION OF ASIAN & AMERICAN ART.

Arthur M. Sackler Gallery

Dr. Arthur M. Sackler (1913–1987), a research physician and medical publisher from New York City, donated 1,000 works of Asian art and $4 million toward construction of the gallery.

MONKEYS GRASP FOR THE MOON

A Chinese folktale tells of monkeys linking tails to retrieve the moon, which they think fell into a well. But the moon's reflection vanishes in the monkey's grasp.

> **Moral:** Those things we work hardest to achieve may be only illusions.

The installation drops 80 feet from the skylight to the lowest floor and is made up of 20 word shapes spelling "monkey" in 21 languages and writing systems. The last monkey is poised over a quiet pool.

PERSIAN

LAO

URDU

MONKEYS
GRASP FOR
THE MOON
(Detail)
BY XU BING
2004

National Museum of African Art
1979

This is the only national museum in the United
States dedicated to the collection, exhibition,
conservation, and study of the arts of Africa.

*GALLERY
SEATING*

ZIGZAG REFERS TO THE ANCESTORS' DIFFICULT PATH.

Mask by Nuna
peoples, Burkina Faso,
mid-20th century
Wood, pigment, metal
2005-6-47. GIFT OF
WALT DISNEY WORLD
CO., A SUBSIDIARY
OF THE WALT DISNEY
COMPANY.

This butterfly mask is so large that it must be
performed by a strong male dancer who can twirl it.
Its design celebrates butterflies, which signal that
the rainy season is coming and the planting season
can begin.

VESSELS FROM THE POTTERY COLLECTION

United States Holocaust Memorial Museum 1993

REMINISCENT OF A CAMP LIGHT

The museum is America's living memorial to the millions who perished in the Holocaust. Architect James Ingo Freed wanted the building, like the exhibit, to "take you in its grip," engaging the visitor's imagination with symbolism that was neither too abstract nor too obvious.

THE HALL OF WITNESS

THE SKYLIGHT, SKEWED & TWISTED WITH FRAGMENTED LIGHT—"TELLS THE VISITOR SOMETHING IS AMISS HERE," FREED SAID.

BRICK, METAL, RIVETS— MATERIALS OF THE PAST?

JEWS WERE NOT ALLOWED ON STREETS & HAD TO USE BRIDGES TO ACCESS GHETTOS.

BLACK & WHITE WALLS AT EACH END— GOOD & EVIL?

STAIRWAY APPEARS TO RECEDE— LIKE A TRAIN TRACK?

35

Bureau of Engraving and Printing
Established 1862

The Bureau of Engraving and Printing is the Department of the Treasury bureau responsible for the printing of US paper money (officially called Federal Reserve Notes).

$

DOLLAR SIGN The origin has many theories—it may derive from the Spanish coat of arms on the piece of eight (which became the US dollar) or from the abbreviation for pesos (Ps), the S written over the P.

PORTRAITS By law, only the dead are honored on bills. Martha Washington was the only woman ($1 silver certificate, 1800's).

FRONT

PAPER IS ACTUALLY 75% COTTON, 25% LINEN.

LINCOLN MEMORIAL

LARGE 5
FOR THE VISUALLY IMPAIRED

PATENT GREEN INK Why the first currency was printed in green is unknown. Perhaps it was readily available, resisted chemical changes, or symbolized stability.

BACK

EMPLOYEES' SIGNS

$ THE BUCK STARTS HERE.

JUST THINK HOW I FEEL, I PRINTED MY LIFETIME SALARY IN A FEW MINUTES.

SMITHSONIAN
National Museum of American History 1964

An ongoing collection of over 3 million objects preserves the memories and experiences of the American people.

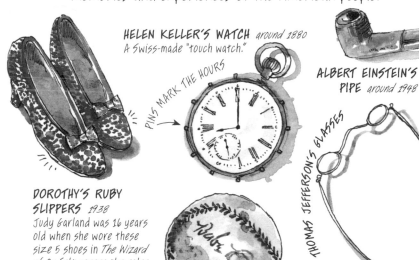

HELEN KELLER'S WATCH *around 1880*
A Swiss-made "touch watch."

PINS MARK THE HOURS

ALBERT EINSTEIN'S PIPE *around 1948*

THOMAS JEFFERSON'S GLASSES

DOROTHY'S RUBY SLIPPERS *1938*
Judy Garland was 16 years old when she wore these size 5 shoes in *The Wizard of Oz.* Felt covers the soles to muffle sound during dance numbers.

BABE RUTH AUTOGRAPHED BASEBALL *around 1930*
The New York Yankees "Sultan of Swat" signed this for a fan in Scranton PA.

MUHAMMAD ALI'S GLOVES *around 1975*
Worn by "the Greatest" while defending the second of his three world heavyweight championships

1.98

MINNIE PEARL'S STRAW HAT *1970's*

37

The Star-Spangled Banner

The National Museum of American History did extensive conservation work on the flag and showcases it in a special gallery within the museum.

History

MARY YOUNG PICKERSGILL, of Baltimore, was paid $405.90 ($3,400 today) by Major George Armistead to sew a garrison flag for Fort McHenry large enough to be seen by British warships. In fact, it was so big that she had to sew it on the floor of a brewery at night.

SEPTEMBER 13, 1814 The British warned Americans that they only had to take down Fort McHenry's flag in surrender to avoid a massive shelling from the sea. They refused and the relentless attack continued throughout the rainy night.

FRANCIS SCOTT KEY, a Washington lawyer arranging a prisoner release with the British, was aboard a ship on the morning of September 14 when he saw that the flag still waved. He was so moved he immediately wrote a poem.

THE NATIONAL ANTHEM The poem was taken to a printer with Key's instructions that it was to be sung to the tune of an old English song. Of the 4 stanzas, only the first is sung.

KEY'S POEM WAS PENNED ON THE BACK OF A LETTER.
(Library of Congress)

the Star Spangled banner.
can ye see by the dawn's early light
oudly we hail'd by the twilight's last gleaming?
stripes, through the clouds of the fight,
the streaming?

STARS 2 FEET IN DIAMETER & CAN BE SEEN FROM BOTH SIDES IN A REVERSE APPLIQUE METHOD

APPLIQUE A MYSTERY. PERHAPS IT IS AN "A" FOR ARMISTEAD.

STRIPES 24" WIDE

ORIGINAL SIZE 30' X 42' 3 STORIES HIGH

15 STARS & STRIPES 1 STAR WAS CUT OUT IN THE 19TH CENTURY.

CURRENT SIZE 30' X 34' OVER 200 SQUARE FEET WAS GIVEN AWAY AS SOUVENIRS BEFORE IT CAME TO THE MUSEUM.

FABRIC Over 400 yards of dyed English wool bunting & white cotton for the stars

LINEN BACKING About 1.7 million stitches were removed in 1998, exposing a side of the flag not seen since 1873 when a backing was attached.

THE ARMISTEAD FAMILY GAVE THE FLAG TO THE SMITHSONIAN IN 1907 ORIGINALLY AS A LOAN.

National Museum of Natural History 1910

This was the first "great museum" to be built on the Mall as proposed by the McMillan Commission. Today the museum, home to over 126 million specimens, has the largest collection in the world.

A TIGER LEAPING OUT OF THE WALL IS A FAVORITE WITH VISITORS.

SCIENTISTS WORK ON DINOSAUR BONES IN OPEN VIEWING LABS.

ALLOSAURUS

THE HOPE DIAMOND
A giant 115-carat diamond was mined in India in the mid 1660's. Over time it was stolen & recut, emerging in 1830 as a 45.52 carat diamond in the collection of Henry Hope. Jeweler Harry Winston acquired it & donated it to the Smithsonian in 1958 by sending it through regular mail in a plain brown paper package.

BUTTERFLIES + PLANTS: PARTNERS IN EVOLUTION
LIVE BUTTERFLIES FROM AROUND THE WORLD

O. ORKIN INSECT ZOO
PET A GIANT MADAGASCAR HISSING COCKROACH

Outdoor Museums

The Smithsonian's secret gardens are tucked away along the Mall to "enhance the overall museum experience of learning, appreciation & enjoyment."

BUTTERFLY HABITAT GARDEN
NATIONAL MUSEUM OF NATURAL HISTORY

HABITAT GARDEN

ENID A. HAUPT GARDEN
BEHIND THE SMITHSONIAN CASTLE

HAUPT GARDEN

MARY LIVINGSTON RIPLEY GARDEN
WEST OF THE HIRSHHORN MUSEUM

KATHERINE DULIN FOLGER ROSE GARDEN
EAST SIDE OF THE ARTS & INDUSTRIES BUILDING

HIRSHHORN MUSEUM & SCULPTURE GARDEN
HIRSHHORN MUSEUM

FOLGER GARDEN

VICTORY GARDEN & HEIRLOOM GARDEN
NATIONAL MUSEUM OF AMERICAN HISTORY

LANDSCAPE GARDENS
NATIONAL MUSEUM OF THE AMERICAN INDIAN
THE NATIONAL AIR & SPACE MUSEUM

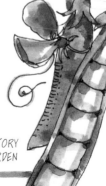

COURTYARD GARDEN
FREER GALLERY OF ART

RIPLEY GARDEN

VICTORY GARDEN

NATIONAL GALLERY OF ART
Sculpture Garden 1999

Over 200 years after Pierre L'Enfant envisioned a landscaped park at 8th Street to mark the city's north-south axis, the Sculpture Garden was dedicated on that site.

AN ENTRANCE TO THE PARIS MÉTROPOLITAIN
1902/1913 by Hector Guimard

Guimard designed 141 historic entrances to the Paris subway system.

METROPOLITAIN

PAVILION CAFÉ

THE CENTRAL FOUNTAIN IS A SKATING RINK IN WINTER.

TYPEWRITER ERASER, SCALE X
1999 stainless steel, plastic, paint
by Claes Oldenburg & Coosje van Bruggen

As a young boy, Oldenburg played with a typewriter eraser in his father's office.

Reblooming iris (summer & late fall) were a favorite of Mrs. Bunny Mellon.

NATIONAL GALLERY OF ART 1941

The museum is actually two distinctive buildings. Andrew W. Mellon donated his collection and funds to build the original West Building. The East Building was designed by I. M. Pei and houses the museum's contemporary collection.

FREE SUNDAY CONCERTS BEGAN IN 1942 FOR THE "THE MEN IN THE ARMED FORCES AND THE WAR-WORKERS IN THE CITY."

The only work by Leonardo da Vinci in the Americas, this portrait of a wealthy Florentine banker's daughter was acquired for the permanent collection in 1967.

Ginevra de' Benci, c. 1474/1478
by Leonardo da Vinci (1452-1519)

At twenty-two, Leonardo was emerging as an innovator in Renaissance painting:

- The three-quarter pose was unusual.

- He experimented with improved oil paints.

- He painted an open land-scape, not a cloistered setting.

- He used more natural subtle shading.

JUNIPER BUSH REPRESENTS CHASTITY AND PUNS THE SUBJECT'S NAME (JUNIPER IS *GINEPRO* IN ITALIAN).

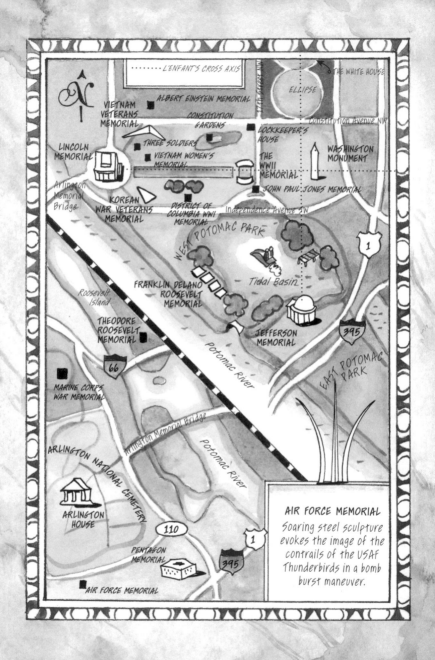

L'ENFANT'S CROSS AXIS

THE WHITE HOUSE

ELLIPSE

17th Street NW

Constitution Avenue NW

VIETNAM VETERANS MEMORIAL

ALBERT EINSTEIN MEMORIAL

CONSTITUTION GARDENS

THREE SOLDIERS

VIETNAM WOMEN'S MEMORIAL

LOCKKEEPER'S HOUSE

THE WWII MEMORIAL

WASHINGTON MONUMENT

LINCOLN MEMORIAL

Arlington Memorial Bridge

KOREAN WAR VETERANS MEMORIAL

DISTRICT OF COLUMBIA WWI MEMORIAL

JOHN PAUL JONES MEMORIAL

Independence Avenue SW

WEST POTOMAC PARK

Tidal Basin

1

FRANKLIN DELANO ROOSEVELT MEMORIAL

Roosevelt Island

THEODORE ROOSEVELT MEMORIAL

JEFFERSON MEMORIAL

395

Potomac River

EAST POTOMAC PARK

66

MARINE CORPS WAR MEMORIAL

Arlington Memorial Bridge

Potomac River

ARLINGTON NATIONAL CEMETERY

ARLINGTON HOUSE

110

PENTAGON MEMORIAL

1

395

AIR FORCE MEMORIAL

AIR FORCE MEMORIAL
Soaring steel sculpture evokes the image of the contrails of the USAF Thunderbirds in a bomb burst maneuver.

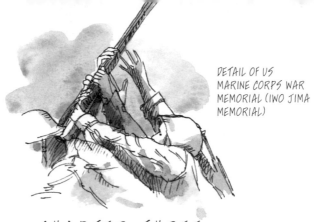

DETAIL OF US
MARINE CORPS WAR
MEMORIAL (IWO JIMA
MEMORIAL)

CHAPTER THREE

MEMORIALS

The original city plan of 1791 called for the Washington Monument to be built on a cross axis of the White House and the Capitol. The soil was too sandy, however, and the monument was built about 100 yards to the southeast.

In the late 1880's, the marsh west of the Washington Monument was filled in all the way to the Potomac, and an artificial tidal basin was created by the reclaimed land of Potomac Park. The Jefferson Memorial was built on a new island in the park (now East Potomac Park) in line with the White House, reestablishing the symmetry lost when the Washington Monument was moved.

PENTAGON MEMORIAL
184 inscribed cantilevered benches, lit below, honor those lives lost on 9/11 at the Pentagon & on American Airlines Flight 77.

FOURTH OF JULY ON THE MALL

WASHINGTON MONUMENT 1884

George Washington, approving L'Enfant's original city plan, thought he would be honored with an equestrian statue, but years later, Congress decided on an Egyptian obelisk that took 36 years to build.

555 FEET LIKE A 45-STORY BUILDING

1858 DUE TO THE CIVIL WAR, WORK STOPPED AT 156 FEET FOR 22 YEARS, SO WHEN BUILDING RESUMED, THE MARBLE WAS A DIFFERENT COLOR.

TWILIGHT TATTOO (May & June)

A sunset military pageant featuring the Old Guard Fife & Drum Corps, the US Army Drill Team & the US Army Jazz Band is held each year at either the Ellipse, Jefferson Memorial, or Fort McNair.

OLD GUARD FIFE AND DRUM CORPS UNIFORMS WERE DESIGNED BY GEORGE WASHINGTON.

The March King

JOHN PHILIP SOUSA (1854-1932) was born in Washington DC and became a famous composer and conductor of American military marches.

Sousa's father, a member of the Marine Band, enlisted his 13-year-old son as an apprentice in the same band. Sousa was raised at Marine Barracks in Washington DC, where he was also schooled in basic subjects by the drum major. He left the band briefly but returned as director of the Marine Band.

SOUSA COMPOSED 136 MARCHES SUCH AS "STARS AND STRIPES FOREVER" "THE WASHINGTON POST" "SEMPER FIDELIS" (Official Marine Corps March)

THE PRESIDENT'S OWN

President Thomas Jefferson gave this title to the Marine Band (the oldest professional musical group—1798), as the band charged with performing for the president.

THE MARINE BAND ALSO PERFORMS FOR THE PUBLIC.

THE LOCKKEEPER'S HOUSE (ca. 1835), one of the oldest houses in DC, sits at the former junction (before landfill) of the Potomac and the Washington Canal branch (Constitution Avenue) of the C&O Canal.

Constitution Gardens 1976

A memorial island in the middle of an artificial lake is dedicated to the fifty-six signers of the Constitution.

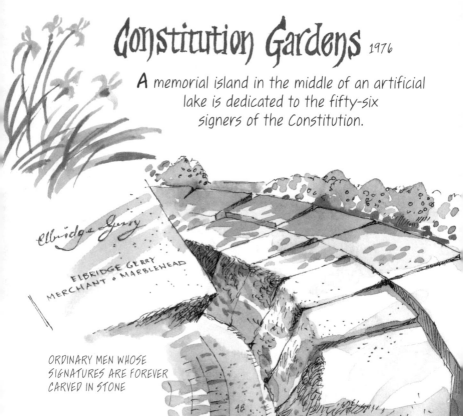

ELBRIDGE GERRY
MERCHANT · MARBLEHEAD

ORDINARY MEN WHOSE SIGNATURES ARE FOREVER CARVED IN STONE

48

Vietnam Veterans Memorial 1982

THE WALL was the winning design, in a national competition, by a young Yale student, Maya Ying Lin. She said, "The names would become the memorial."

SYMBOLS

+ (PLUS SIGN) MISSING IN ACTION

◆ CONFIRMED DEAD

◈ MIA CONFIRMED DEAD

GRANITE FROM INDIA, CUT IN VERMONT & ETCHED IN TENNESSEE.

OVER 58,250 NAMES NEW NAMES ARE ADDED IF THEY MEET ELIGIBILITY REQUIREMENTS.

THREE SOLDIERS
by FREDERICK HART (Detail)

"I see the wall as a kind of ocean, a sea of sacrifice... I place these figures upon the shore of that sea... reflecting the human face of it, the human heart."
—FREDERICK HART

VIETNAM WOMEN'S MEMORIAL
by GLENNA GOODACRE (Detail)

The kneeling woman may be the heart & soul of the statue because so many can identify with her.

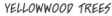

YELLOWWOOD TREES
REPRESENTING THE MILITARY WOMEN WHO DIED, THESE TREES SEEM TO WEEP IN THE SPRING.

THE **WORLD WAR II MEMORIAL** 2004

A national memorial to the spirit, sacrifice, and commitment of the American people, united together in a common and just cause for peace and freedom from tyranny.

FREEDOM WALL 4,000 gold stars represents over 400,000 Americans who gave their lives.

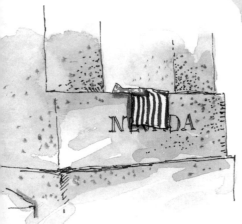

56 PILLARS Represent states (including the District of Columbia) and territories at the time of the war. Beginning with the first state, Delaware, pillars alternate to the right and left of the Freedom Wall, depending on when they entered the Union.

KILROY WAS HERE

A popular expression in WWII. American servicemen would leave the doodle wherever they went and it became a part of popular culture. (Hint: it is behind a gate on the SW side of the memorial.)

LINCOLN MEMORIAL 1922

In designing the 19-foot-tall seated statue, sculptor Daniel Chester French studied Mathew Brady's photographs of Lincoln. It took the Piccirilli brothers of New York four years to carve it under French's direction.

FASCES BIRCH STICKS BOUND TOGETHER WITH A RED RIBBON WERE ROMAN SYMBOLS OF POWER & STRENGTH THROUGH UNITY.

A

L

IS LINCOLN USING SIGN LANGUAGE TO SPELL HIS INITIALS?

No. During Lincoln's presidency, casts were made of his hands in a closed position. Daniel Chester French studied the casts & designed the right hand slightly open to give the statue more life.

Korean War Veterans Memorial 1995

Five years after World War II, America joined 22 other nations under the UN flag to defend South Korea against communism. Inscriptions summarize the true meaning of the memorial:

> OUR NATION HONORS HER SONS AND DAUGHTERS WHO
> ANSWERED THE CALL TO DEFEND A COUNTRY THEY NEVER KNEW
> AND A PEOPLE THEY NEVER MET

FREEDOM IS NOT FREE

KOREAN NATIONAL FLOWER ROSE OF SHARON BUSHES ARE ON THE SOUTH SIDE.

THIS ARMY ASSISTANT GROUP LEADER & THE SQUAD ON PATROL SEEM TO BE CONVERSING.

OVER 7 FEET TALL

GRANITE WALL BY LOUIS NELSON, WITH IMAGES REPRESENTING 1.5 MILLION AMERICANS INVOLVED IN THE WAR

HARSH WEATHER WINDBLOWN PONCHOS

RUGGED TERRAIN REPRESENTED BY GRANITE STRIPS & JUNIPER BUSHES

NUMBER **38**

- 38TH PARALLEL WAS BORDER BETWEEN NORTH & SOUTH KOREA.
- 19 REFLECTIONS IN THE WALL=38 STATUES.
- WAR LASTED 38 MONTHS.

19 STAINLESS STEEL STATUES EACH SIGNED BY SCULPTOR FRANK GAYLORD, A WWII VETERAN

52

Tidal Basin 1880's

RECREATION PADDLEBOATS FOR RENT

The Tidal Basin was created to keep the Washington Channel free of debris. An inlet gate from the Potomac River and outlet gate to Washington Channel open and close with the tides, flushing the channel.

FISHING RECORD IS A 58-POUND CARP

OCCASIONALLY, BEAVERS HAVE GOTTEN INTO THE TIDAL BASIN & FELLED A FEW CHERRY TREES.

JAPANESE PAGODA (1600)
PRESENTED BY THE MAYOR OF YOKOHAMA IN HONOR OF THE 1858 HARRIS TREATY OF "PEACE, AMITY & COMMERCE"

JAPANESE CHERRY TREES MORE THAN 3,700 RING THE 1.72-MILE WALKWAY.

53

Cherry Blossom Time

The original idea of planting cherry trees in DC came from travel writer Eliza Ruhamah Scidmore, who returned from Japan in 1885 with a suggestion that cherry trees be planted along the proposed reclaimed Potomac waterfront.

She lobbied for 27 years, and in 1912 Japan gave 3,020 Yoshino cherry trees to First Lady Helen Taft as a symbol of the friendship between Japan and the US.

In 1965, Japan gave First Lady Lady Bird Johnson another 3,800 trees. The circle of friendship continued in 1981, when America gave cuttings of the original trees back to Japan to replace the parent trees lost in a flood.

Life is short
like the three-day glory
of the cherry blossom
— traditional Japanese haiku

BIRD FOOD
TREES PRODUCE
A BITTER
PEA-SIZE CHERRY.

YOSHINO CHERRY
WHITE SINGLE BLOOM

THERE ARE ABOUT 50-80
ORIGINAL TREES LEFT. DUE
TO SOIL COMPACTION BY FOOT
TRAFFIC THE LIFE SPAN IS NOW
ABOUT 50 YEARS.

KWANZAN CHERRY
ROSY DOUBLE BLOOM

NATIONAL CHERRY BLOSSOM FESTIVAL

Two weeks of festivities celebrate spring and Japan's gift of the cherry trees. Cultural performances, sporting events, arts and crafts demonstrations, and other special events culminate with a parade along Constitution Avenue.

LIGHTING OF THE JAPANESE LANTERN (1651) AT THE TIDAL BASIN IS A CEREMONIAL HIGHLIGHT OF THE FESTIVAL.

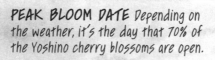

PEAK BLOOM DATE Depending on the weather, it's the day that 70% of the Yoshino cherry blossoms are open.

SAKURA MEANS "CHERRY BLOSSOMS."

SAKURA MATSURI JAPANESE STREET FESTIVAL

The largest one-day street festival of Japanese culture in America features Japanese and Asian food, Japanese products at the Ginza Marketplace, martial arts demonstrations, cultural exhibitions, and more.

J-POP LAND
YOUNG, MODERN PERFORMING ARTS

TRADITIONAL PERFORMING ARTS

Franklin Delano Roosevelt Memorial 1997

Franklin D. Roosevelt (1882-1945) said that if the nation insisted on a memorial then it should be "no bigger than my desk." He got that (outside the National Archives) plus a 7.5-acre memorial divided into outdoor "rooms" with works by artists depicting his four terms.

THE TWO ROOSEVELT STATUES

PROLOGUE ROOM Robert Graham's sculpture was added at the request of disability activists.

Although life-size, Roosevelt seems small.

FDR DESIGNED HIS OWN WHEELCHAIR USING:

A KITCHEN CHAIR (FOR COMFORT)

BICYCLE WHEELS

TRICYCLE WHEELS

ROOM 3 Sculptor Neil Estern depicts Roosevelt as a larger-than-life commander-in-chief during WWII.

DISABILITY SYMBOL: CHAIR HAS CASTORS.

FALA

MILITARY CAPE DISGUISES FDR'S DISABILITY.

STRAP IS PART OF HIS POLIO BRACE.

ROOSEVELT'S SCOTTISH TERRIER SYMBOLIZES HIS GOOD HUMOR IN THE FACE OF ADVERSITY.

JEFFERSON MEMORIAL
1943

Thomas Jefferson
(1743- 1826)
wrote his own
epitaph before
dying on July 4:

*Author of the Declaration
of American Independence,
of the Statute of Virginia
for Religious Freedom, and
father of the University of
Virginia.*

Jefferson omitted being
the third president and
some unusual achievements:

- He knew six languages.
- He invented the wooden
  coat hanger, swivel
  chair, sliding door, the
  dumbwaiter, and more.
- He introduced broccoli
  to America and made
  tomatoes popular.

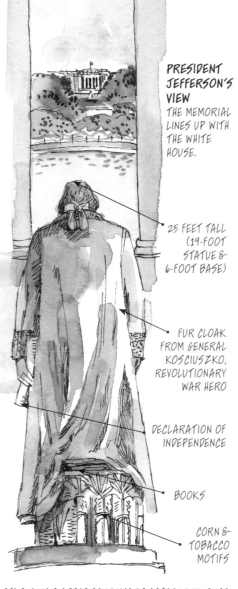

**PRESIDENT
JEFFERSON'S
VIEW**
THE MEMORIAL
LINES UP WITH
THE WHITE
HOUSE.

25 FEET TALL
(19-FOOT
STATUE &
6-FOOT BASE)

FUR CLOAK
FROM GENERAL
KOSCIUSZKO,
REVOLUTIONARY
WAR HERO

DECLARATION OF
INDEPENDENCE

BOOKS

CORN &
TOBACCO
MOTIFS

STATUE WAS ADDED FOUR YEARS AFTER WWII, ONCE
A BAN ON CIVILIAN USES OF BRONZE WAS LIFTED.

Theodore Roosevelt Island

1967

NATIONAL MEMORIAL

A MOAT
SURROUNDS
THE OUTDOOR
MEMORIAL.

THE ISLAND
ABOUNDS WITH
WILDLIFE AND
TRAILS.

This wooded island memorial aptly honors President Theodore Roosevelt (1858-1919), naturalist & conservationist. His many quotes about nature, manhood, youth & the state are inscribed on four large stone tablets.

NATURE
"There is delight in the hardy life of the open."

ISLAND NAMES IN HISTORY:
Analostan—Native Americans fished here.
My Lord's Island—Island given to Lord Baltimore
Barbadoes—Owned by a sea captain
Mason's Island—Family owned for 125 years

GRAY FOX

PILEATED WOODPECKER

HONEYSUCKLE

DEER

(Animals drawn at the National Museum of Natural History.)

BALLS STAMPED WITH THE PRESIDENTIAL SEAL

68

Hidden Treasures

Off The beaten path, these memorials are worth the treasure hunt.

JOHN PAUL JONES MEMORIAL (1912)

Potomac Park's first monument is a tribute to the Revolutionary War naval hero best known for his quote, "Surrender? I have not yet begun to fight!"

ALBERT EINSTEIN MEMORIAL
(1979)

Sculptor Robert Berks also created the bust of John F. Kennedy at Kennedy Center.
The celestial map at the foot of this giant Einstein plots 2,700 identified stars & their position at noon, April 22, 1979—the moment the statue was dedicated.

DISTRICT OF COLUMBIA
WWI MEMORIAL (1931)

Once a popular bandstand holding an 80-piece band, the memorial honoring the citizens of DC who served in WWI is now a quiet temple among the azaleas.

THE ROBERT E. LEE MEMORIAL

Arlington House 1803

George Washington Parke Custis built his home as a museum to honor the grandparents who raised him, George and Martha Washington. His daughter, Mary, married Robert E. Lee and became the guardian of the family's heritage.

Lee's family had been in Virginia for 200 years, so when civil war broke out, General Lee decided to resign from the Union Army to defend Virginia, leaving Arlington Plantation forever.

THE PORTICO'S MASSIVE DORIC COLUMNS ARE ACTUALLY FAUX MARBLED ON STUCCOED BRICK.

SELINA GRAY
GAINED FREEDOM IN 1862.

WASHINGTON TREASURY

The war forced Mary Lee to evacuate Arlington, leaving the house and Washington treasures in the capable hands of her personal slave, Selina Gray. The collection of portraits and letters were shipped away and other items locked in the cellar. When Union troops moved into the house, Selina discovered heirlooms missing and confronted General McDowell. Because of her efforts, Washington's artifacts were moved to the patent office for safekeeping and exhibition and returned to the Lee family 40 years later.

Arlington National Cemetery 1864

During the war, when Mary Lee failed to appear in person (new law) to pay her property taxes, Arlington's 1,100 acres were confiscated and the government started a military grave-yard. In 1882 the Lees' son and heir won his suit to return the family estate. But by then, hundreds of graves covered the hills and he took the government's offer of $150,000 for the property.

TOMB OF THE UNKNOWNS Interred are unknown soldiers from WWI, WWII & the Korean War. The Vietnam crypt is now empty after the soldier was identified & reinterred near his home.

FREEDMAN'S VILLAGE A camp for fugitive & freed slaves became a functional village. 3,800 graves mark the area. (Section 27)

JFK GRAVESITE When asked where she wanted her husband buried, Jackie Kennedy replied, "He belongs to the people."

PIERRE L'ENFANT'S TOMB The first city planner was reinterred outside Arlington House. But his birth date & rank are wrongly inscribed & his name was written as "Pierre" instead of "Peter," as he preferred to be called.

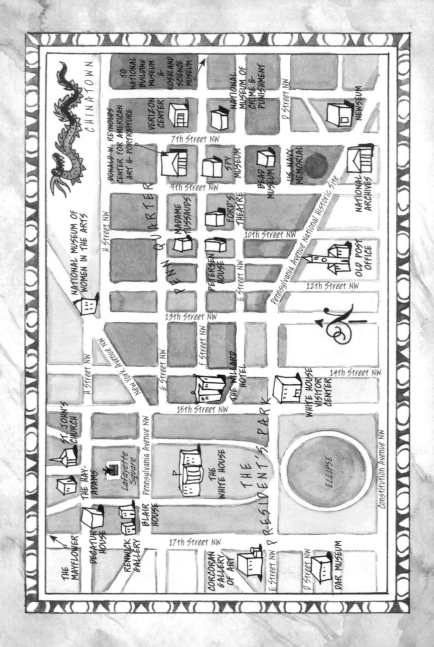

CHAPTER FOUR

THE PRESIDENT'S PARK & DOWNTOWN

When city architect Pierre L'Enfant was asked why he placed the President's House so far down Pennsylvania Avenue from the Capitol, he responded, "Presidential messages should be delivered to congress with decorum, thus requiring time and therefore distance."

President Kennedy said Pennsylvania Avenue had become unworthy of an inaugural parade route, so in 1965 it was revitalized and the avenue became a National Historic Site.

Downtown has been revived with a thriving cultural and entertainment district in Penn Quarter and Chinatown.

STREET LAMP IN CHINATOWN

DAR Museum Founded 1890

Daughters of the American Revolution (DAR) is a lineage society dedicated to patriotism, historic preservation, and education. It was founded by four women whose ancestors were patriots of the American Revolution.

DAR LIBRARY RESEARCH YOUR LINEAGE IN THIS VICTORIAN WEDDING-CAKE ROOM CROWNED WITH A SKYLIGHT.

MEMBERSHIP ELIGIBILITY Any woman 18 years or older who can prove lineal descent from a patriot who fought, fed the troops, supplied goods or money, or served in the new government.

FROM THE LARGE QUILT COLLECTION
PRINCESS FEATHERS BY DOROTHY HENRIETTA SCHARFF CARLE, 1840-1850, PITTSBURGH PA

PERIOD ROOMS SPONSORED BY 31 STATES THE WEST VIRGINIA ROOM REPRESENTS AN EARLY 19TH-CENTURY PARLOR SERVING AS A SCHOOLROOM.

BEFORE BUILDING HIS GALLERY, CORCORAN OPENED HIS HOME & COLLECTION TO VISITORS TWICE A WEEK. IN FACT SOME OF THE GALLERY ROOMS FEEL LIKE A HOME.

Corcoran Gallery of Art Founded 1869

William Wilson Corcoran (1798-1888) of Georgetown was building a gallery (what is now the Renwick Gallery) for his collection when the Civil War erupted and halted construction. The gallery finally opened in 1874 but the collection and the art school it spawned outgrew the building. A new Beaux-Arts building was built and the old one was sold to the US Government.

LIONS GUARD THE DIVERSE COLLECTION OF PHOTOGRAPHY & MEDIA ARTS, DECORATIVE ARTS, EUROPEAN & CONTEMPORARY ART & HISTORIC AMERICAN ART.

GRAND SALON
AN ELEGANT 4,300 SQ. FT. RE-CREATION OF A 19TH-CENTURY COLLECTOR'S PICTURE GALLERY

PAINTINGS ARE HUNG SALON STYLE, 40 FEET FROM FLOOR TO CEILING.

Visitors listen to an artist lecture.

SMITHSONIAN AMERICAN ART MUSEUM'S
Renwick Gallery 1861

This originally private art gallery of Washington banker and philanthropist William Wilson Corcoran was named for its architect, James Renwick Jr., who also designed the Smithsonian Castle. In the 1950's when the French Second Empire-style Renwick was to be torn down, First Lady Jackie Kennedy led the effort to save this gem, which was later given to the Smithsonian. Today the gallery collects, exhibits, studies, and preserves American crafts and decorative arts from the 19th to 21st centuries.

Grand Hotels

THE WILLARD HOTEL 1850. "The Residence of Presidents" has hosted every president in some way since its opening. Here, Kentucky Senator Henry Clay mixed the city's first mint julep at the Round Robin bar; Julia Ward Howe wrote the "Battle Hymn of the Republic"; President Ulysses S. Grant popularized the term *lobbyist* when he was approached by those with special interests while enjoying a brandy and cigar in the lobby; and Martin Luther King Jr. completed his famous "I Have a Dream" speech here.

MINT JULEP IS THE WILLARD'S SIGNATURE DRINK.

THE MAYFLOWER 1925. A RENAISSANCE HOTEL "The Grand Dame of Washington DC" was said to be decorated with more gold than any building in the country, except for the Library of Congress.

COLUMN DECORATION IN 24K GOLD LEAF

THE HAY-ADAMS 1928. "Where nothing is overlooked but the White House." This Italian Renaissance hotel was named after John Hay (President Lincoln's secretary) and Henry Adams (great-grandson of President John Adams), whose homes were on this site across from Lafayette Park and the White House.

BOUQUETS AWAIT GUESTS.

HOW MOST VISITORS SEE
THE WHITE HOUSE.

The White House 1800

BLUE ROOM
After the fire of
1814, James Monroe
purchased this set
of furniture from
French cabinetmaker
Antoine Bellangé.
(White House Visitor Center)

The "Presidential Palace," as critics called it, was the first public building to be constructed in the new city. Irish-born architect James Hoban won the design competition (Thomas Jefferson submitted an anonymous entry) and worked closely with President Washington, who did not live to see it completed. John Adams was the first to live here.

In the War of 1812, British soldiers set fire to the mansion, badly damaging it. Hoban was called upon to rebuild the President's House, and later added the north and south porticoes. Theodore Roosevelt made the name White House official on his stationery in 1901.

****

The China Room

President Truman said, "It seems like there's always somebody for supper." Until Mrs. Benjamin Harrison began collecting china (1889) from previous administrations, it was sold, given away or destroyed. Today, it is displayed in the China Room.

JAMES POLK
(1845-1849)

JAMES MONROE (1817-1825)
This was the first service designed for the exclusive use by an American president.

ABRAHAM LINCOLN (1861-1865) The Solferino color chosen by Mary Todd Lincoln was criticized as "royalist."

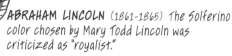

RUTHERFORD B. HAYES (1877-1881) This most distinctive china featured etchings of American game, fowl, fish, and plants.

WOODROW WILSON (1913-1921) The Wilsons had Lenox make the first American-made presidential china.

HARRY S. TRUMAN (1945-1953) The Williamsburg green band matched the State Dining Room walls.

RONALD REAGAN (1981-1989) Nancy Reagan's signature red was chosen under candlelight.

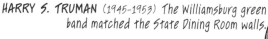

LYNDON B. JOHNSON (1963-1969)
Lady Bird Johnson had plates designed with wildflowers from each state and DC.

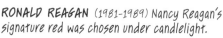

First Ladies

As the most famous women in America, many first ladies have been advocates for a variety of social causes.

DOLLEY MADISON A girls orphanage

MARY TODD LINCOLN Housing, employment, and the education of freed slaves

HELEN "NELLIE" TAFT Workplace conditions and a health and safety law

FLORENCE HARDING Treatment of animals

ELEANOR ROOSEVELT Civil rights and social reform

JACKIE KENNEDY Historic preservation

LADY BIRD JOHNSON Environmental protection

PAT NIXON Volunteerism

BETTY FORD Equal rights for women

ROSALYNN CARTER Care for the mentally ill

NANCY REAGAN Drug prevention among young people

BARBARA BUSH Literacy

HILLARY CLINTON Health care

LAURA BUSH Education and libraries

WORN BY MARY TODD LINCOLN (1861–1865)
(National Museum of American History)

DETAIL FROM NEIL ESTERN'S STATUE OF ELEANOR ROOSEVELT
(FDR Memorial)

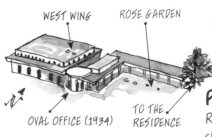

WEST WING

ROSE GARDEN

OVAL OFFICE (1934)

TO THE RESIDENCE

N

The Oval Office
1909

President Taft expanded Teddy Roosevelt's west wing and changed the shape of his office to an oval like the famous Blue Room. The oval rooms in the Residence were inspired by George Washington's practice of greeting guests assembled in a circle.

THE RESOLUTE DESK

In 1853 the Royal Navy's *HMS Resolute* was abandoned in the Arctic ice. The ship drifted for two years until it was found by an American whaler. It was then refitted and returned to Queen Victoria as a gift from President Franklin Pierce and the American people. When *Resolute* was retired in 1879, Victoria ordered a desk to be made from its timbers and given to President Rutherford B. Hayes.

FDR DID NOT LIVE TO SEE THE MODESTY PANEL HE ORDERED.

THE 2-INCH BASE WAS ADDED TO ACCOMMODATE FDR'S WHEELCHAIR.

OVAL OFFICE RUG
RECENT PRESIDENTS HAVE SELECTED INDIVIDUAL RUG DESIGNS FOCUSING ON THE PRESIDENTIAL SEAL.

The Grounds

SEASONAL FLOWERS ARE ALSO PLANTED IN THE ROSE GARDEN.

THE ROSE GARDEN Edith Roosevelt created a colonial garden, but In 1913, Ellen Wilson replaced it with a rose garden. During the Kennedy years, friend Bunny Mellon created the current Rose Garden with space for ceremonies.

CHILDREN GET A WOODEN EGG FROM THE PRESIDENT & FIRST LADY.

EASTER EGG ROLL The Easter tradition began on the South Lawn with President & Mrs. Rutherford B. Hayes in 1878. The day is full of festivities including the popular egg rolling event.

NATIONAL CHRISTMAS TREE ON THE ELLIPSE The festivities on the Ellipse begin with the lighting of the tree. Fifty-six smaller trees are lit daily for the fifty states, territories, and District of Columbia.

1923—FIRST LIGHTING WAS BY CALVIN COOLIDGE.
1978—A LIVE TREE WAS PLANTED AND IS STILL USED TODAY.
1995—TREE LIT WITH SOLAR ENERGY.

First Pets

> "If you want a friend in Washington, get a dog."
> —*HARRY S. TRUMAN*

First Families have had more than 400 pets, including some unusual ones:

THOMAS JEFFERSON was given a magpie from the Lewis & Clark expedition.

TAD LINCOLN had a turkey named Jack.

THEODORE ROOSEVELT'S family had more pets than any other president, including Maude the pig.

WILLIAM TAFT'S Holstein, Pauline Wayne, was the "queen of capital cows."

WOODROW WILSON had sheep mowing the lawn during WWI & the wool was sold as a fund-raiser for the Red Cross.

CAROLINE KENNEDY was given Macaroni the Pony by Lyndon Johnson.

FIRST PET BOOKS

FRANKLIN D. ROOSEVELT'S dog, Fala, was the subject of the first presidential pet biography.

HILLARY CLINTON'S cat in *Dear Socks, Dear Buddy.*

BARBARA BUSH'S dog in *Millie's Book.*

73

Lafayette Square

This leafy park was, at various times, a family graveyard, apple orchard, and market before becoming a park for the President's House. During Jefferson's presidency, Pennsylvania Avenue cut through the park, making the surrounding blocks available for private ownership. President's Park was renamed for General Lafayette on his 1824 visit.

A SHADY PARKING PLACE.

ANDREW JACKSON (1853) The other two casts of this statue are in New Orleans and Nashville. He is the only American in the park. The other statues are American Revolutionary War heroes from Europe.

BLAIR HOUSE (1824) The official state guest house of the president is a complex of four connected townhouses, and, at 70,000 square feet, is larger than the White House.

President's Park had become a very fashionable area to live in early 1800. Architect Benjamin Latrobe designed the Decatur House, St. John's Church, and helped Dolley Madison with the President's House interiors and furnishings.

BANISTER NEWEL AT DECATUR HOUSE

THE STEPHEN DECATUR HOUSE MUSEUM (1818)

The first house on the block is now one of the oldest homes in the city. Naval hero Stephen Decatur built his home for lavish entertaining, but 14 months later, he was killed in a duel. His wife, Susan, auctioned their belongings and moved to Georgetown. Over the years, it has been rented to dignitaries, sold, occupied (army in the Civil War), and finally bequeathed by the last owner, Marie Beale, to the National Trust.

THE 54TH PEW IS RESERVED FOR THE PRESIDENT. NEEDLEPOINT STOOLS HONOR THE PRESIDENTS.

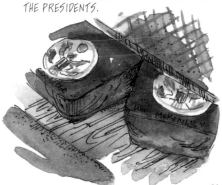

ST. JOHN'S EPISCOPAL CHURCH (1815)

Built in the form of a Greek cross, this was the first building in the park. James Madison and every president since has worshipped here at the "Church of the Presidents."

75

Pennsylvania Avenue
NATIONAL HISTORIC SITE

AMERICA'S MAIN STREET Pennsylvania Avenue has been a ceremonial way from the Capitol to the White House ever since Thomas Jefferson's second inauguration in 1805. But the street is only part of this national park.

WHITE HOUSE VISITOR CENTER

The center offers opportunities to learn more about the White House and the presidency through exhibits, artifacts, videos, park ranger talks, and special events.

"Faux bamboo" side chair from a White House bedroom (1873-1881) was returned to the collection in 1995.

OLD POST OFFICE 1899

Saved from destruction, the building has been revitalized with shops and a food court under a glass atrium. The tower houses Ten Bells of Congress, a gift from England, that are replicas of those in Westminster Abbey. They are rung by a volunteer group on special occasions and can be viewed from the observation deck.

NEWSEUM

2008

TV NEWS
HELICOPTER

The First Amendment is displayed outside on a 50-ton marble tablet confirming that the world's most interactive museum is dedicated to journalism & free speech.

NEWSPAPERS
DISPLAYED
OUTSIDE
DAILY

BE A TV REPORTER
CHOOSE A BACKDROP
& READ FROM THE
TELEPROMPTER.

FIVE FREEDOMS OF THE FIRST AMENDMENT
Freedom of Religion
Freedom of Speech
Freedom of the Press
Right to Assemble
Right to Petition

REPORTER'S
PENCIL
CA. 1860's

Civil War reporters & artists carried a notebook, binoculars, watercolor set & a flask!

BERLIN WALL
EIGHT 12-FOOT-HIGH SECTIONS PLUS
AN EAST BERLIN GUARD TOWER THAT
WAS NEAR CHECKPOINT CHARLIE

9/11 GALLERY
ALL THAT IS LEFT OF THE
BROADCASTING ANTENNA
MAST THAT WAS ATOP THE
NORTH TWIN TOWER

The National Archives 1935

The nation's "safety deposit box" preserves permanently valuable government records & grants public access to those documents.

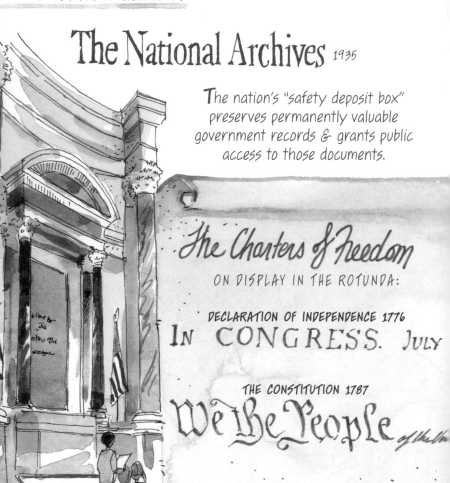

The Charters of Freedom

ON DISPLAY IN THE ROTUNDA:

DECLARATION OF INDEPENDENCE 1776

IN CONGRESS. JULY

THE CONSTITUTION 1787

We the People of the U

THE BILL OF RIGHTS 1789

Congress of the United St

The Archives displays facsimile sketches of the Great Seal of the United States (1782). It took the Continental Congress six years and three committees to agree on one. The State Department keeps the brass seal to emboss about 2,000-3,000 official documents a year.

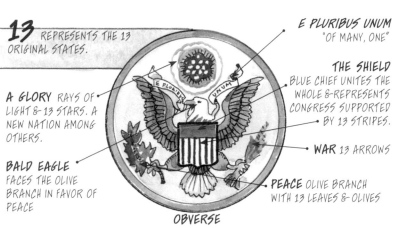

13 REPRESENTS THE 13 ORIGINAL STATES.

E PLURIBUS UNUM "OF MANY, ONE"

THE SHIELD BLUE CHIEF UNITES THE WHOLE & REPRESENTS CONGRESS SUPPORTED BY 13 STRIPES.

A GLORY RAYS OF LIGHT & 13 STARS. A NEW NATION AMONG OTHERS.

WAR 13 ARROWS

BALD EAGLE FACES THE OLIVE BRANCH IN FAVOR OF PEACE

PEACE OLIVE BRANCH WITH 13 LEAVES & OLIVES

OBVERSE

EYE & MOTTO THE EYE OF PROVIDENCE & "PROVIDENCE FAVORS"

52 LETTERS ON THE WHOLE SEAL ARE DIVISIBLE BY 13.

UNFINISHED PYRAMID (13 STEPS) STRENGTH & DURATION

RIBBON 13 SIDES SHOWING

1776 SIGNING OF THE DECLARATION OF INDEPENDENCE

MOTTO SIGNIFIES THE NEW AMERICAN ERA

REVERSE OR SPIRITUAL SIDE

BOTH SIDES OF THE GREAT SEAL ARE ON THE REVERSE OF THE ONE-DOLLAR BILL.

On Stage

Some theaters offer kid-friendly & free events.

ARENA STAGE
Pioneer of the regional theater movement

FOLGER THEATRE
Shakespeare's plays performed in the Elizabethan Theatre

MACBETH

FORD'S THEATRE
Entertainment in a historic setting

HARMAN CENTER FOR THE ARTS
The Shakespeare Theatre Company performs at
Sidney Harman Hall & the Lansburgh Theatre.

THE KENNEDY CENTER
A president's living memorial for
music, dance & drama

NATIONAL THEATRE
May be haunted by John McCullough, said to
have been murdered backstage by a fellow actor

MILLENNIUM STAGE
AT THE KENNEDY
CENTER HAS FREE
PERFORMANCES
EVERY DAY.

THE STUDIO THEATRE
Its mission is to produce the best in
contemporary theater.

WARNER THEATRE
This historic theater offers theatrical,
dance & television presentations

WOOLLY MAMMOTH THEATRE
Experience the leading edge of theater.

McCULLOUGH

AUDITIONING AT WOOLLY
MAMMOTH THEATRE

Offbeat Museums
Penn Quarter has some
unusual educational museums.

National Building Museum 1985
Changing exhibits in this 1887 Pension Building show every American can play a part in the continual improvement of our built environment.

INFECTIOUS DISEASES

MARIAN KOSHLAND
Science Museum 2004
OF THE NATIONAL ACADEMY OF SCIENCES

This interactive museum engages visitors in current scientific issues that impact our lives.

The Bead Museum 1995

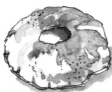

FOSSILIZED SEA
URCHIN 5000 BCE

Founded by the Bead Society of Greater Washington, the museum's bead timeline of history identifies beads geographically from 10,000 BCE to present. The museum also has temporary exhibits, an extensive bead library, and a gift shop.

SELF-TOUR
NUMBERS ARE
REFERENCE
GUIDES TO
EACH BEAD'S
CATALOGED
STORY.

243

264

246

254

249

260

Power Dining

Washington DC is a political town with powerful people dining in legendary powerhouse places:

BISTRO BIS
Sophisticated French cuisine, it's "where Capitol Hill dines."

BULLFEATHERS OF CAPITOL HILL
"Serving the House of Representatives and all their friends."

THE DUBLINER RESTAURANT AND PUB
A spirited Irish pub with a vast selection of beers and ales

THE MONOCLE RESTAURANT
The "first table cloth restaurant" on the Hill (1960's)

THE OCCIDENTAL RESTAURANT
Since 1906, it's "where statesmen dine."

OLD EBBITT GRILL
"The oldest saloon in Washington" since 1856

THE OVAL ROOM
A virtual "who's who" dine here in elegance.

PALM RESTAURANT
One of the oldest family-owned restaurants in America

40-FOOT BAR AT BULL-FEATHERS

BEER STEIN COLLEC-TION AT OLD EBBITT GRILL

"SCREAMING MIMI" DRINK AT THE PALM

NATIONAL MUSEUM OF

CRIME&PUNISHMENT 2008

THE CRIME SCENE

An interactive museum of America's history of crime and punishment and the crime-fighting heroes. Test your skills at a simulated FBI shooting range and high-speed police chase. Crack a safe, hack a computer, or solve a crime from clues at a "real-life" crime scene, working on the CSI unit with forensic science technology.

THE "DEATH CAR" FROM THE MOVIE *BONNIE & CLYDE* WAS DELIVERED THROUGH THE MUSEUM'S SECOND-FLOOR WINDOW.

AL CAPONE'S HOMEY ALCATRAZ CELL (1934-1938)

DISTRESSED PLASTER WALLS

HARRY HOUDINI'S ORIGINAL PADLOCK

AMERICA'S MOST WANTED VISITORS CAN WATCH THIS TV CRIME-FIGHTING SERIES' CALL CENTER LIVE EVERY SATURDAY AT 6PM IN THE MUSEUM'S STUDIO.

veri*z*on Center
1997

A sports and entertainment facility with 220 world-class sporting events, concerts, and family shows annually. The arena has executive suites and a basketball practice court and is located among shops, restaurants, and movie theaters.

SCOREBOARD CENTER HUNG HIGH-DEFINITION LED

HOME TO:

WASHINGTON MYSTICS (WNBA)

WASHINGTON WIZARDS (NBA)

GEORGETOWN HOYAS (NCAA)

WASHINGTON CAPITALS (NHL)

DC AREA STADIUMS

NATIONALS PARK
Home to the Washington Nationals (MLB)

ROBERT F. KENNEDY MEMORIAL STADIUM
Home to the DC United (MLS)

FEDEXFIELD (Landover MD)
Home to the Washington Redskins (NFL)

HIGH-DEFINITION SCOREBOARD IS 4,811 SQUARE FEET (47 FEET HIGH).

NATIONALS PARK 2008

Located on the Anacostia River south of the Capitol, this is the first LEED-certified (Leadership in Energy and Environmental Design) green ballpark in America. It is the home of Major League Baseball's Washington Nationals and seats 41,888 fans.

ENERGY
THE 6,300 SQ. FT. SEDUM (LOW SUCCULENT PLANT) "GREEN ROOF" MINIMIZES HEAT GAIN.

RECYCLING
ON-SITE RECYCLING OF GLASS, METAL, PLASTIC, CARD-BOARD, AND PAPER PRODUCTS

ALTERNATIVE TRANSPORTATION
SUBWAY, BUSES, AND BIKES ARE ENCOURAGED.

NATURE
KWANZAN CHERRY TREES IN CENTER-FIELD PLAZA

BIKE RACK

SMITHSONIAN AMERICAN ART MUSEUM 1829
and
THE NATIONAL PORTRAIT GALLERY 1968

The two museums are in a National Historic Landmark building and collectively known as the Donald W. Reynolds Center for American Art and Portraiture.

THE KOGOD COURTYARD

BILLOWING GLASS CANOPY

BLACK OLIVE TREES

WATER FEATURE IS A THIN PLANE OF WATER ON THE GRANITE FLOOR.

ANDREW JACKSON
replica of 1836 original by Ferdinand Pettrich

GEORGE WASHINGTON, 1796
by Gilbert Stuart

This is the second Washington portrait by Stuart. Commissioned by Martha Washington for herself, it was left unfinished so Stuart could use it as a model for other commissions. It is also the image engraved on the $1 bill.

Within the museums are two unique public spaces.

Luce Foundation Center for American Art

A three-story, open study/ storage facility densely displays over 3,000 paintings, sculptures, and a wide variety of art objects from the SAAM collection.

STORAGE TREASURES

Lunder Conservation Center

Floor to ceiling glass windows show conservators from both museums at work.

PAINTINGS STUDIO

Grime, darkened varnish, and old, discolored retouching are carefully removed. Lost paint areas are filled with gesso and inpainted without covering any of the artist's original paint.

FRAMES STUDIO
PRESERVES & REBUILDS FRAMES

DENTAL TOOLS ARE USED FOR DELICATE WORK.

BEFORE

AFTER

MISS SATTERLEE
by Charles Bird King
oil on wood,
ca. 1830-1839

International Spy Museum 2002

This popular interactive museum has the largest collection of international spy-related artifacts on public display and is the first museum dedicated solely to espionage.

KISS OF DEATH
Lipstick pistol, Russian KGB ca. 1965, 4.5mm single-shot weapon

CANISTER WITH SECRET MESSAGES

FLY, SPY!
In WWI pigeons were fitted with cameras to take pictures of enemy positions.

PUMPKIN PAPERS
Three rolls of microfilm were found in a hollowed pumpkin on famous spy Whitaker Chambers's family farm.

SCENT JARS
The East Berlin Stasi chief kept jars of scents from several thousand suspects in case dogs needed to track them.

CIGARETTE PISTOL & COMPONENTS
Single-shot .22 caliber

Madame Tussauds
2007 ★

Marie Grosholtz (1761–1850) was a child apprentice to Dr. Philippe Curtius, a wax modeler in Paris who had a museum of life-size wax figures. When he died, Marie inherited the exhibition, which she took on tour for 33 years under her married name.

MARIE'S LAST WORK WAS A SELF-PORTRAIT, 1842.

CRAFTSMANSHIP

Each figure takes about four months to complete, then grooming & hair washing is done regularly.

BODY Made of durable fiberglass

HEAD Made of delicate wax

HAIR Inserted strand by strand

EYES Hand painted (10 hours) acrylic with veins of red silk thread.

TEETH Each tooth is individually made & colored

CLOTHES & ACCESSORIES Donated by celebrities or copied

FIRST LADY JACKIE KENNEDY

Ford's Theatre 1863
NATIONAL HISTORIC SITE

About 10:00 p.m., April 14, 1865

Five days after the South had surrendered, President Lincoln sat watching a performance of *Our American Cousin* when John Wilkes Booth, actor and Confederate sympathizer, stepped into the box and shot Lincoln in the back of the head. Booth then jumped from the box, catching his spur in a flag, and broke his leg on the stage. He fled on horseback but was later cornered in a Virginia barn and shot.

THE STATE BOX

MARY TODD LINCOLN SAT NEXT TO HER HUSBAND WITH 2 GUESTS IN THE BOX.

GEORGE WASHINGTON'S PICTURE WAS PLACED IN LIEU OF A PRESIDENTIAL SEAL, WHICH DID NOT YET EXIST.

PRESIDENT LINCOLN SAT IN A PLUSH ROCK-ING CHAIR.

SOME THINGS LINCOLN HAD WITH HIM WHEN HE WAS SHOT:
(Library of Congress)

Repaired with a string!

2 PAIRS OF GLASSES

POCKET KNIFE

9 NEWSPAPER CLIPPINGS

$5 CONFEDERATE NOTE!

TOP HAT
(National Museum of American History)

PETERSEN HOUSE

Mortally wounded, Lincoln was attended by Dr. Leale and carried out into the street, where Henry Safford, a boarder at the Petersen rooming house, was holding a candle and crying out, "Bring him in here, bring him in here."

"The giant sufferer" was so tall (6' 4") that he was laid diagonally on the bed. (The original bed is owned by the Chicago American History Museum.)

7:22:10 a.m., April 15, 1865

Lincoln never regained consciousness. Dead at the age of 56, he was the first president to be assassinated.

Chinatown

Locals call this area "China-block" because the neighborhood has dwindled considerably. But in an effort to preserve the Asian character, local laws dictate that new businesses must have signs in English and Chinese.

FRIENDSHIP ARCHWAY (1986)
A traditional Chinese gate designed by a local architect celebrates the friendship with Beijing, DC's sister city. A plaque claims it is the largest such archway in the world.

NESH NUUDLE MADE

CHINATOWN HAS A FEW CHINESE BUSINESSES & ABOUT 20 CHINESE AND ASIAN RESTAURANTS.

星巴克咖啡

STARBUCKS

NATIONAL MUSEUM of WOMEN in the ARTS
1981

In the 1960's Wilhelmina Cole Holladay and Wallace F. Holladay began collecting works by women artists. Women had been underrepresented in museum collections, and it was Mrs. Holladay's dream to create a woman's museum. Today, the Holladay Collection is the core of the permanent collection.

THE MUSEUM WON ARCHITECTURAL AWARDS FOR ITS INTERIOR REDESIGN OF A MASONIC TEMPLE.

LILLY MARTIN SPENCER
(American, 1822-1902)

Thanks to her parents' efforts, Spencer was a trained artist. While her husband managed the household and 13 children, she became the family's principal breadwinner. In the late 1840's and 1850's, Spencer's still lifes, portrait paintings, and humorous domestic genre scenes were popular in Europe and America.

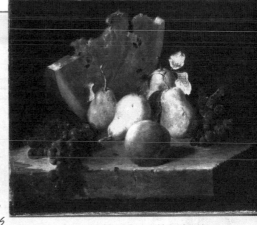

STILL LIFE WITH WATERMELON, PEARS AND GRAPES
ca. 1860
oil on canvas, 13 1/8 x 17 1/4 inches

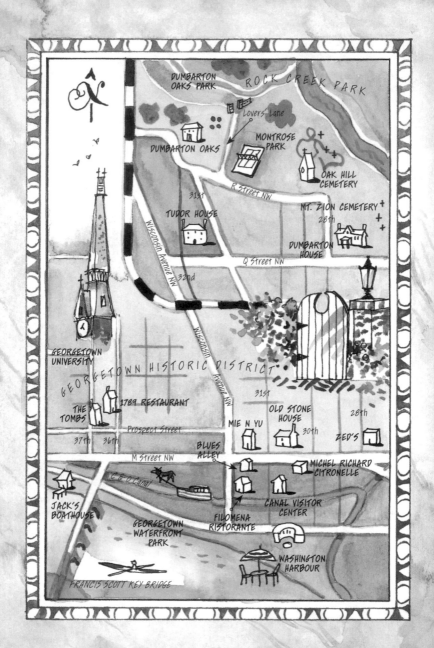

DUMBARTON HOUSE
A FEDERAL
PERIOD HISTORIC
HOUSE MUSEUM
CA. 1800

CHAPTER FIVE

GEORGETOWN

In 1751 George Beall and George Gordon founded the Town of George, in what was then Maryland. It was named either for King George II or for its founders and became Georgetown.

Georgetown was the farthest point ocean-going boats could navigate on the Potomac River and it grew into a wealthy, thriving port for transferring goods, especially tobacco, to boats on the C&O Canal.

The Canal Company went bankrupt in the 1890's and the area declined until after the Depression. In the 1950's Senator John F. and Jackie Kennedy lived here, helping to restore Georgetown's reputation as a fashionable neighborhood.

CALL BOXES FOR THE POLICE AND FIREMEN IN THE LATE 1800'S HAVE BEEN RESTORED AS ART PROJECTS.

Old Stone House 1765

One of the oldest preserved homes in the city thanks to a myth that George Washington and Pierre L'Enfant met here to plan the new capital, Old Stone House was originally built as a one-room, lower-middle-class house for the Layman family. The father died before the house was completed, leaving a will that listed carpenter tools, bedsteads, chests, one towel, two Pennsylvania Dutch Bibles, and one table but no chairs.

The house was sold to Cassandra Chew, a wealthy widow, who added a rear kitchen and second floor.

BLUE FIELDSTONE WALLS ARE 2-3 FEET THICK & THERE ARE PIT SAW MARKS ON THE OAK BEAMS.

WHAT USED TO BE A CAR LOT IN BACK IS NOW A PEACEFUL ENGLISH GARDEN.

Georgetown Historic District

Following the Civil War, 19th-century brick row houses were popular because they were economical to build. A typical row house might be 24′ long by 12′ wide, with a garden in the back.

ROD STARS

Before the Civil War, two-story structures were held together by an iron pole through each end of the building and secured with a decorative tie rod.

ROW HOUSES ALONG THE HISTORIC C&O CANAL

DC Universities

AMERICAN UNIVERSITY 1893
Promoting international understanding

THE CATHOLIC UNIVERSITY OF AMERICA 1887
The national university of the Catholic Church

CORCORAN COLLEGE OF ART AND DESIGN 1890
Washington's only college of art and design

GALLAUDET UNIVERSITY 1864
A leader in deaf education for over a hundred years

GEORGETOWN UNIVERSITY 1789
The nation's oldest Catholic and Jesuit university

THE GEORGE WASHINGTON UNIVERSITY 1821
A private research institution

HOWARD UNIVERSITY 1867
Played a large role in American history and
the civil rights movement

SOUTHEASTERN UNIVERSITY 1879
A private, nonprofit learning institution

UNIVERSITY OF THE DISTRICT OF COLUMBIA
1974   A historically black public university

HOWARD UNIVERSITY

GALLAUDET
UNIVERSITY

Georgetown UNIVERSITY 1789

What began as Georgetown College with 12 students and a few professors now has 4 undergraduate schools, graduate programs, a law school, and a medical school. The vision of its founder, John Carroll, still guides the university in its commitment to Catholic, Jesuit education in the liberal arts tradition.

THE TOMBS IS A FAVORITE HOYA LOCAL PUB.

GEORGETOWN UNIVERSITY FOUNDER, ARCHBISHOP JOHN CARROLL

JOHN CARROLL FOUNDER

HOYA LORE

GEORGETOWN HOYAS The university's sports teams were originally nicknamed "the Stonewalls," but it's thought that a student, using Greek and Latin terms, started the cheer "Hoya Saxa!" or "What Rocks!" Now all the university's teams carry the name.

BLUE & GRAY Georgetown adopted its official colors in 1866, symbolizing the union of the North and South following the Civil War.

C&O Canal NATIONAL HISTORICAL PARK

Completed 1850

George Washington's dream of a commercial waterway connecting Chesapeake Bay and the Ohio River was realized when President John Quincy Adams broke ground on this twelve-year, $4.5 million canal running 340 miles from Georgetown to Pittsburgh. Twenty-two years and about $14 million later, its 184.5 miles only reached Cumberland MD.

PARK RANGER IN PERIOD COSTUME

WORK GLOVES

NATIONAL PARK RANGERS OFFER MULE-DRAWN BARGE RIDES THROUGH THE HEART OF TOWN.

By the time the canal opened, it was obsolete, as railroads had flourished in those twenty-two years. However, the canal continued to operate until 1924.

CANAL LOCKS ARE NUMBERED 0-75 WITH NO LOCK 65.

LOCK 4

TIGHT SQUEEZE
LOCKS: 100' LONG X 15' WIDE
BOATS: 95' LONG X 14.5' WIDE

Waterfront Property

JACK'S BOATHOUSE

A family-operated canoe, kayak, and rowboat rental business since WWII.

GEORGETOWN WATERFRONT PARK

What once was a parking lot has been transformed into a 10-acre green space overlooking the Francis Scott Key bridge.

WASHINGTON HARBOUR

A scenic setting of condominiums, office space, boat docks, and a wide public boardwalk with restaurants offering seasonal outdoor dining

THE MALLARD IS A DABBLE DUCK.
dab·ble to feed on shallow-water vegetation with rapid, splashing movements of the bill

Dining in G'Town

Georgetown is rich in history, shopping, and dining diversity.

BLUES ALLEY An intimately casual jazz supper club

BLUES ALLEY

FILOMENA RISTORANTE Old World Italian cooking in an extraordinary setting

MICHEL RICHARD CITRONELLE An award-winning chef creates his own French modern and witty cuisine.

MICHEL RICHARD IN CITRONELLE'S EXHIBITION KITCHEN

MIE N YU A blend of Asian, Middle Eastern, European, and Mediterranean cuisines in a fanciful setting

"THE SILK ROAD" FUNKY DECOR AT MIE N YU

1789 RESTAURANT Five elegant, romantic, and antique-filled dining rooms

ZED'S Traditional Ethiopian dishes served up in a unique dining experience.

ZED WONDEMU, OWNER OF ZED'S

1789 RESTAURANT

"PASTA MAMA" AT FILOMENA RISTORANTE

TUDOR PLACE 1816

This suburban villa was built above the wharf by Martha Washington's granddaughter Martha Custis and her husband, Thomas Peter. Layers of history are reflected in items that have been cherished by five generations over three centuries.

WASHINGTON'S CAMP STOOL

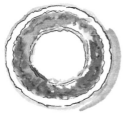

59 DIFFERENT SETS OF CHINA

THE GARDEN'S 200-YEAR OLD TULIP POPLAR IS DC'S "MILLENNIUM LANDMARK TREE."

1700's George & Martha Washington's possessions from this period were later given or sold to family.

1816 The Peters have 140 pieces of Washington memorabilia, making theirs the largest collection second only to Mount Vernon.

1844 Britannia Peter Kennon inherited Tudor & lived here for 92 years.

1914 Armistead Peter Jr. bought out his siblings & began a modernization of Tudor.

1960 Armistead Peter 3rd inherited the home & lived here until 1983. He created the Tudor Place Foundation to preserve its memories.

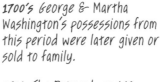

"OLD BLUSH" ROSE FIRST PLANTED BY MARTHA CUSTIS PETER

BRITANNIA'S CANDLESTICK

Resting Places

Montrose Park

In the early 1900's a group of women petitioned Congress to purchase this land from rope-making magnate Robert Parrott and establish a recreational park.

Dumbarton Oaks 1920

Mildred & Robert Woods Bliss hired Beatrix Farrand to create the formal gardens around their mansion. The museum and gardens are open to the public.

FORSYTHIA HILL

Dumbarton Oaks Park

The Blisses donated 27 acres of their property for a public park.

Oak Hill Cemetery 1849

When William Corcoran (Corcoran Gallery of Art) purchased this track of land known as Parrott's Woods, he was influenced by the "rural cemetery" movement of a land-scaped countryside combined with English gardens creating a park to be enjoyed by the living.

GOTHIC CHAPEL DESIGNED BY JAMES RENWICK JR. USING THE SAME RED SANDSTONE TRIM HE USED IN THE SMITHSONIAN CASTLE

UNUSUAL MASONRY

Mount Zion Cemetery 1808 & 1842

The old Methodist Burying Ground and the Female Union Band Society Graveyard were adjacent cemeteries that combined to form this cemetery of slaves and free blacks. Mount Zion United Methodist Church was a historically black congregation, and members of the Female Union Band Society were free black women committed to helping each other in sickness and in death.

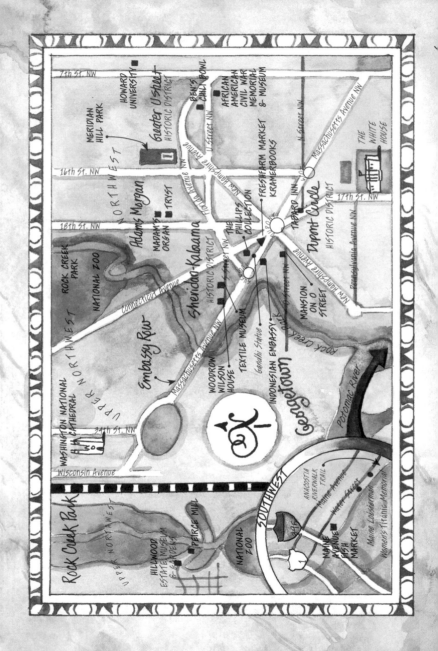

CHESS UNIVERSITY OF DUPONT CIRCLE WHERE THE HOMELESS AND A LOCAL CHESS KING GIVE LESSONS IN THE PARK

CHAPTER SIX

NEIGHBORHOODS

Following the Civil War, Washington DC was inundated with freed blacks, veterans, widows, and government workers. To accommodate this population explosion, the infrastructure was improved, roads were paved, and row houses were built. The invention of the streetcar helped expand the city beyond L'Enfant's original Boundary Street (Florida Avenue).

Today, the Metro system allows visitors to easily get beyond the city's memorials and museums to discover the distinctive flavors of its historic, architecturally unique, multicultural neighborhoods.

A LOCAL SECRET, THE TABARD INN IS THE LONGEST CONTINUALLY OPERATED HOTEL IN DC, WITH SUNDAY JAZZ AND CHARMING INDOOR AND PATIO DINING.

RESTORED VICTORIAN-ERA
ROW HOUSES

Greater U Street Historic District

BEN'S CHILI BOWL
THIS HEART & SOUL OF
THE NEIGHBORHOOD
SINCE 1958 IS FAMOUS
FOR ITS CHILI DOGS.

The neighborhood of Shaw began as a camp for freed slaves during the Civil War. It was named after Colonel Robert Shaw, commander of the first official black unit in the US military. It became known as a "city within a city" and was a vibrant center of African-American intellectual and cultural life—U Street's jazz clubs were known nationally as "Black Broadway." In 1968 Shaw began to decline but successful renewal efforts focused on preserving its residential character.

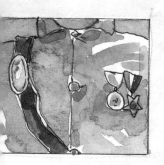

THE AFRICAN AMERICAN CIVIL WAR MEMORIAL & MUSEUM
Honoring African Americans' heroic struggle for freedom & civil rights

THE SPIRIT OF FREEDOM
MEMORIAL LISTS THE NAMES
OF 209,145 SOLDIERS WHO
SERVED IN THE US COLORED
TROOPS REGIMENTS OF
THE CIVIL WAR.

Duke Ellington 1899–1974

Edward Kennedy Ellington lived near U Street. He was always well dressed and said it was a chum who called him "Duke" to lend them both class.

At age seven he began taking piano lessons but quit in favor of baseball and art. Then he met ragtime pianist Harvey Brooks, who inspired him to play with expression and freedom. As a teenager, Ellington wrote the first of 2,000 compositions and started his own band.

Ellington brought elegance and style to the international music world and to the U Street club scene, which hosted all the great jazz notables.

(Courtesy Madame Tussauds Museum)

"Playing 'bop' is like playing Scrabble with all the vowels missing."

"I merely took the energy it takes to pout and wrote some blues."

"My band is my instrument even more than the piano."

A FEW OF ELLINGTON'S INSIGHTFUL QUOTES

SCORE FROM "SATIN DOLL"

HOWARD
UNIVERSITY 1867

In 1862 Civil War refugees and ex-slaves living in Shaw were given refuge and treated at a freedmen's hospital in a converted army barracks at Camp Barker.

After the war, this freedmen's hospital was relocated to Howard University, newly founded for African Americans. The Freedmen's Hospital would later come to support the university's famed College of Medicine.

FOUNDERS LIBRARY
CLOCK TOWER

HOWARD HALL 1869
This National Historic Landmark was one of the first buildings on campus and was home to Oliver O. Howard, a Civil War general and one of the founders of Howard University.

Meridian Hill PARK
1936

GLOVES IN WINTER

THE DRUM CIRCLE
Every Sunday afternoon for 40 years, drummers & other musicians have gathered at the top of the hill to play while crowds dance to the rhythms.

Commodore David Porter named his estate Meridian Hill (ca. 1815) as it was on L'Enfant's north-south axis with the White House. By midcentury, the grounds had become a pleasure park, and during the Civil War, Union troops encamped there. The government purchased the property in 1910 and created a Neoclassicist American park. Because of the park's unique design and exposed aggregate concrete, it is a National Historic Landmark managed by Rock Creek Park.

FOUNTAIN CASCADES INTO THIRTEEN BASINS.

Dupont Circle Historic District

Dupont traffic circle is an example of Pierre L'Enfant's vision for the city—grand avenues radiating off small parks like spokes on a wheel. However, he could not have envisioned the trendy, vibrant neighborhood that has become Dupont Circle.

KRAMERBOOKS & AFTERWORDS CAFE & GRILL IS ONE OF MANY CULTURAL LANDMARKS.

FRESHFARM MARKETS
There are several seasonal markets in DC, but the Dupont Circle market is open every Sunday.

THE MANSION ON O STREET

This DC secret is a luxury B&B, a museum, conference center, and private club, yet offers spectacular dining and entertaining events for the public.

The Mansion is actually five interconnected townhouses (32 secret doors) and overflows with serious treasures and quirky artifacts. And everything is for sale, including entire rooms!

FROM SUNDAY BRUNCH TO MONDAY MARTINI MADNESS.

THE PHILLIPS COLLECTION 1921

America's first museum of modern art was founded by Duncan Phillips (1886–1966), who displayed his personal art collection in the intimate spaces of his 1897 Georgian Revival mansion. Since then, the museum has added two additions and now holds one of the finest collections of European and American art from the 19th, 20th, and 21st centuries.

Phillips purchased works from unknown artists & students for his "encouragement collection."

DAUGHTER & SON OF THE PROPRIETOR

EX-MAYOR OF SAIGON

ACTRESS

POET

EDITOR

BUREAUCRAT

ARTIST

ITALIAN JOURNALIST

ACTRESS

SEAMSTRESS & RENOIR'S FUTURE WIFE

SAILOR/ ARTIST

In *Luncheon of the Boating Party* (1880–1881), Pierre-Auguste Renoir painted idealized portraits of his friends and colleagues on the balcony of the Maison Fournaise, a boat rental, restaurant, and small hotel overlooking the Seine.

Sheridan-Kalorama Historic District

These neighborhoods are part of what once was the hilltop Kalorama (Greek for "beautiful view") estate overlooking the city. This residential area is also known for its Embassy Row mansions.

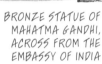

THE TEXTILE MUSEUM MAGNIFYING GLASS WITH MUSEUM LOGO FOR VIEWING THE INTERNATIONAL TEXTILE COLLECTION

BRONZE STATUE OF MAHATMA GANDHI, ACROSS FROM THE EMBASSY OF INDIA

EMBASSY ROW Dozens of embassies line Massachusetts Avenue NW. The Embassy of the Republic of Indonesia was once the home of Evalyn Walsh McLean, the last private owner of the Hope Diamond (see *National Museum of Natural History*).

WOODROW WILSON HOUSE 1915

In 1921 the twenty-eighth president, Woodrow Wilson, and his wife, Edith, returned from the White House to private life in this house. Upon Mrs. Wilson's death in 1961 and at her bequest, the house and its contents came to the National Trust for Historic Preservation and so the house remains today as it was when they lived here.

Woodrow Wilson (1856-1924) was the first and only president to earn a doctoral degree and the second to win a Nobel Peace Prize. During Wilson's term, the Federal Reserve System, League of Nations, Internal Revenue Service, women's right to vote, and the observance of Mother's Day were established.

BALL SIGNED BY KING GEORGE V IN WILSON'S DUGOUT ROOM

A GRADUATE OF PRINCETON UNIVERSITY, WILSON WAS ITS FIRST LAY (NONMINISTER) PRESIDENT.

THE MASTER BED Wilson suffered a stroke before moving here. To make him comfortable, Edith had this bed made with the same dimensions as the Lincoln bed he had slept in for eight years. Wilson also died in this bed.

ADAMS MORGAN

Once a fashionable suburb, the neighborhood declined during World War II until desegregation, when immigrants arrived. A new name for the neighborhood was chosen by combining the names of two area schools—the all-black Thomas P. Morgan Elementary School and the all-white John Quincy Adams Elementary School.

Today this is one of the city's most multicultural, "happening" neighborhoods with a great ethnic restaurant scene.

ANIMAL CRACKER

TRYST COFFEEHOUSE AND BAR A café coexisting with a lounge bar in a room filled with comfy thrift-shop furniture

MADAM'S ORGAN BLUES BAR & SOUL FOOD RESTAURANT Its mural is a neighborhood icon and its slogan legendary: "Where the beautiful people go to get ugly."

Rock Creek Park 1890

Rock Creek Park is one of the oldest parks in the National Park Service and one of the largest forested urban parks in America, with 1,755 acres along the Rock Creek Valley. Rock Creek Historic District also has another 1,000 acres scattered across northwest DC, including Meridian Hill Park and Old Stone House in Georgetown.

Since 1904 this dam blocked the path of fish returning from the Atlantic Ocean to spawn. Now a new fish "ladder" allows fish to swim upstream.

WHITE PERCH

ALEWIFE

PEIRCE MILL 1820

Isaac Peirce built this water-powered grist mill on Rock Creek, along with a house, barn, and other buildings. When the parks department purchased the estate in 1890, the family continued operation, but in 1897 the main drive shaft broke and the family abandoned the mill.

National Zoo 1889

Orang Xing

This 163-acre zoo and park was planned by Secretary of the Smithsonian Samuel Langley, conservationist William Temple Hornaday, and landscape architect Frederick Law Olmsted. Together they designed a zoo that would not only exhibit animals but also serve as a refuge for threatened wildlife.

FUJIFILM GIANT PANDA HABITAT
HOME FOR PANDA PAIRS SINCE 1972

CHEETAH CONSERVATION STATION
THE FASTEST MAMMAL (OVER 70 MPH) IS DISAPPEARING.

AMAZONIA HABITAT AND SCIENCE GALLERY
GRANT'S STAG BEETLE FROM CHILE

INVERTEBRATE EXHIBIT
PURPLE SEA STAR

KIDS' FARM
"LUCY" THE NIGERIAN DWARF GOAT

ASIA TRAIL
SLOTH BEARS EAT TERMITES AND LOVE HONEY.

HILLWOOD

ESTATE, MUSEUM & GARDENS 1955

Wealthy heiress Marjorie Merriweather Post purchased this estate overlooking Rock Creek Park and began to refurbish it to showcase her renowned collection in an intimate setting.

GREENHOUSE ORCHIDS

Today this estate museum includes the most comprehensive collections of 18th- and 19th-century Russian imperial art outside of Russia, as well as one of the world's most important collections of 18th-century French decorative arts.

GARDEN LAMP

ROSE GARDEN

JAPANESE-STYLE GARDEN

This traditional interpretation of a mountain scene is a blend of authentic Japanese garden style and American practicality.

WATERFALL

PONDS ARE CONNECTED BY STREAMS AND WATER-FALLS.

THE MINIATURE MOUNTAINSIDE IS MADE UP OF 500 BOULDERS.

GOLDFISH

Washington National Cathedral 1907

OFFICIAL NAME: Cathedral Church of Saint Peter and Saint Paul.

CONSTRUCTION: Exactly 83 years (September 29, 1907–September 29, 1990).

SIZE: Sixth largest cathedral in the world and second largest in America, behind Saint John's in New York City.

INTERRED: Woodrow Wilson (only president buried within DC) and Helen Keller, among 150 others.

LAST SERMON: Days before he was assassinated, Rev. Dr. Martin Luther King Jr. preached his last Sunday sermon here.

SPACE WINDOW
A LUNAR ROCK FROM THE ASTRONAUTS OF APOLLO XI IS EMBEDDED HERE.

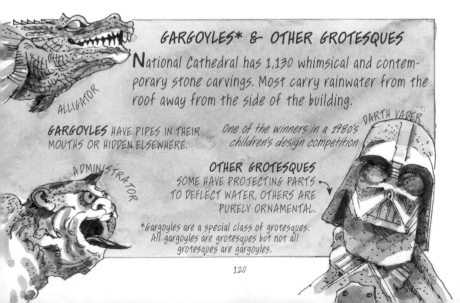

GARGOYLES* & OTHER GROTESQUES

National Cathedral has 1,130 whimsical and contemporary stone carvings. Most carry rainwater from the roof away from the side of the building.

ALLIGATOR

GARGOYLES HAVE PIPES IN THEIR MOUTHS OR HIDDEN ELSEWHERE.

One of the winners in a 1980's children's design competition

DARTH VADER

ADMINISTRATOR

OTHER GROTESQUES
SOME HAVE PROJECTING PARTS TO DEFLECT WATER, OTHERS ARE PURELY ORNAMENTAL.

*Gargoyles are a special class of grotesques. All gargoyles are grotesques but not all grotesques are gargoyles.

Washington Channel

The open air Maine Avenue Fish Market, one of the oldest of its kind, was thriving in George Washington's day. Originally, boats brought produce and seafood up the Potomac every 3 days, but with the invention of iced trucks, "buy boats" remained docked here. Eventually, they were replaced by steel barges that support the many stalls where locals and visitors can sit, stand, and mingle while eating fresh seafood.

CAPTAIN WHITE'S SEAFOOD CITY

A CAST OF CRABS

ANACOSTIA RIVERWALK TRAIL

A 20-mile multiuse trail along the Anacostia River that, when completed, will connect 16 waterfront neighborhoods from the Tidal Basin to the Bladensburg Waterfront Park in Prince George's County MD.

THE MAINE LOBSTERMAN
In 1939 a lobster trapper posed for this sculpture by Victor Kahill.

BOULDER

THE WOMEN'S TITANIC MEMORIAL
"To the brave men who perished in the wreck of the *Titanic* April 15, 1912. They gave their lives that women and children might be saved."
Erected by the Women of America

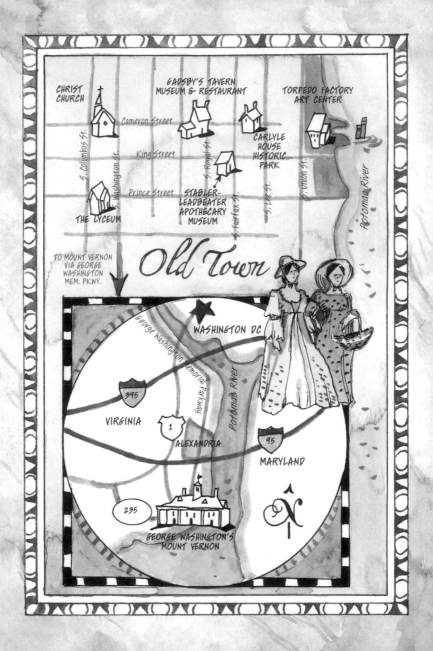

CHRIST
CHURCH

GADSBY'S TAVERN
MUSEUM & RESTAURANT

TORPEDO FACTORY
ART CENTER

Cameron Street

King Street

CARLYLE
HOUSE
HISTORIC
PARK

Prince Street

STABLER-
LEADBEATER
APOTHECARY
MUSEUM

THE LYCEUM

S. Columbus St.

S. Washington St.

S. Royal St.

S. Fairfax St.

S. Lee St.

S. Union St.

Potomac River

TO MOUNT VERNON
VIA GEORGE
WASHINGTON
MEM. PKWY.

Old Town

WASHINGTON DC

George Washington Memorial Parkway

Potomac River

395

VIRGINIA

1

ALEXANDRIA

95

MARYLAND

235

GEORGE WASHINGTON'S
MOUNT VERNON

N

CHAPTER SEVEN

ALEXANDRIA & MOUNT VERNON

Alexandria's Old Town historic district was a thriving international shipping port and eventually a suburb of the new Federal Capital across the Potomac. It was also George Washington's hometown. He was a town trustee, sold his farm products at the port, and launched military campaigns from town.

When George Washington inherited the Mount Vernon farms, he spent so much time in Alexandria for business and pleasure that he and Martha built a town house to avoid traveling the eight miles back to the Mansion House Farm.

"FIRST PERSONS" AT MOUNT VERNON ARE
INTERPRETIVE PERFORMERS, REPRESENTING
FRIENDS, FAMILY, AND SLAVES.

123

Christ Church 1773

George Washington and Robert E. Lee were actively involved in Alexandria's first Episcopal church. Traditionally, each US president attends a service here, and visitors can sit in Washington's pew.

PEW #59
ONLY GEORGE & MARTHA WASHINGTON'S PEW (PURCHASED FOR ABOUT $1,000) HAS BEEN PRESERVED IN THE ORIGINAL CONFIGURATION.

HAND-LETTERED TABLETS

Two original hand-painted tablets on either side of the wine-glass pulpit contain the Apostles' Creed, Ten Commandments, and Lord's Prayer. The words were painted on a white background by the building's architect, Col. James Wren, and have never been retouched, although the background has mellowed to gold.

AMEN.

STABLER-LEADBEATER APOTHECARY MUSEUM

Edward Stabler's successful apothecary sold a wide range of goods, from medicines to furniture polish.

SHOW GLOBES in bright colors were originally window advertising for the apothecary.

John Leadbeater married one of Stabler's sixteen children, and the Leadbeater family operated the business from 1852–1933, when the Depression forced them to close. At auction, the building and contents were preserved by local community efforts and today a wealth of inventory continues to be discovered and cataloged.

MOUNT VERNON PERFUME was a line developed by Leadbeater.

REGULAR CUSTOMERS Robert E. Lee purchased lavender for his headaches and Martha Washington bought castor oil one month before she died.

JOB'S TEARS have a natural hole at each end and are thought to have been strung as teething rings. A dusty drawer still stores the seeds.

HOUSE PAINT Robert E. Lee ordered his paint here.

E. S. LEADBEATER & SONS' PAINTS

THE MUSICIAN'S BALCONY IN THE BALLROOM

Gadsby's Tavern Museum CA. 1785 & 1792

Innkeeper John Gadsby leased the City Hotel in 1796 and the adjoining tavern soon after. The establishment quickly became the center of political, social, and business activities.

The Assembly Room above the ca. 1785 tavern was used for entertainment and by visiting vendors, dentists, portrait painters, etc. to market their wares and talents. The Ballroom in the 1792 City Hotel was the site of the famous Birthnight Ball held in honor of George Washington's birthday (he and Martha attended in 1798 and 1799) and Thomas Jefferson held his inauguration here in 1801.

RUM PUNCH THE TAVERN SPECIALTY WAS DRUNK FROM BOWLS.

Today, Gadsby's Tavern Restaurant is open to the public for lunch and dinner, where you can still order Surrey County Peanut Soup and Sally Lunn bread served on replicas of period dishes.

George Washington Ate Here

The original tavern's private dining room, reserved for important gentlemen, was the only room in which women were allowed to dine.

SALLY LUNN BREAD
A cakelike bun perhaps named after an English girl or from the French *sol et lune* (sun & moon).

MADEIRA WINE
It's said the taste of this Portuguese wine & brandy mixture improved when jostled in a ship's hold & heated by the sun.

CANVASBACK DUCK

POTOMAC ROCK FISH

CHESAPEAKE BAY OYSTERS

PEANUT SOUP
A FAVORITE OF GEORGE WASHINGTON'S

OVERSIZED NAPKINS

WHITE TABLECLOTHS & FINE CHINA

JOHN CARLYLE SENT SHELLS TO HIS
BROTHER GEORGE IN ENGLAND TO
SHOW HIM THE NATIVE FLORA & FAUNA
OF VIRGINIA.

SWAN NECK MOLDINGS

PERIOD-STYLE
FLOOR CLOTH

Carlyle House Historic Park 1753

John Carlyle (1720–1780) was a Scots-man who came to Virginia as a factor (representative) for an English merchant. He married Sarah Fairfax, and their home was the center of social and political life in Alexandria, due in part to friends like George Washington (related by marriage). One visitor was British General Braddock, who made the man-sion his headquarters for three weeks to plan the French and Indian War.

THE 18TH-CENTURY-STYLE GARDEN WITH PLANTINGS FROM JOHN CARLYLE'S TIME

Torpedo Factory Art Center 1918

Originally built as the US Naval Torpedo Station for the manufacture of torpedoes in both world wars, the complex was later used as storage space for the Smithsonian's dinosaur bones and art objects as well as congressional records. In 1969 the city bought the buildings and later renovated them by creating studios and galleries for artists.

HALL SINK

This Mark XIV torpedo was made here in 1945 and was brightly painted so that it could be found in the water when it was tested.

Today the Torpedo Factory is one of the most successful visual arts centers in America, featuring professional artists working and exhibiting their work.

ORIGINAL PECAN TREE

GEORGE WASHINGTON'S
Mount Vernon
ESTATE & GARDENS 1765

George Washington's 8,000-acre Mount Vernon Plantation was actually five farms. The Mansion House Farm, where he and his family lived, is what we call Mount Vernon today.

The cupola's windows open as a ventilator to cool the house. After the war, Washington added a dove of peace weathervane.

In the 1670's, his great-grandfather acquired this estate, then George inherited it from his half-brother, who named the property Mount Vernon after his commanding officer in the British navy, Admiral Edward Vernon.

Washington chose most of the interior paint colors, including this popular yet expensive verdigris for the dining room.

130

President & Lady Washington

GEORGE WASHINGTON (1732-1799)

Land surveyor at 16, commander-in-chief of the Continental Army at 43, and first president of the United States at 57, this remarkable man, a farmer at heart, finally retired at 65 and died in his bed from a throat ailment at 67.

45 YEARS OLD Using computers, forensic anthropologists created wax figures of Washington at ages 19, 45 & 57.

MARTHA CUSTIS WASHINGTON

(1731-1802) She described herself as "an old-fashioned Virginia housekeeper, steady as a clock, busy as a bee and cheerful as a cricket."

A widow with two children, Martha married Colonel George Washington on January 6, 1759, and moved to Mount Vernon in April. They were away during most of the war and presidential years, returning here forever on March 15, 1797.

REPLICA OF MARTHA'S
GOLD BROCADE
WEDDING DRESS

THE TIDEWATER GENTLEMAN FARMER

The father of our country took great pride in being a farmer and spent 45 years innovatively designing and planting the gardens at Mount Vernon while keeping detailed journals.

FIGS
Washington said he was happy to leave public life & retire "under the shadow of my own Vine & Fig tree."

DOGWOOD
Trees that bloomed were dubbed by Washington as "clever trees."

WHEAT
He changed from the traditional tobacco crops to this more stable and lucrative one.

SEED HOUSE
He loved to experiment with exotic plants from seeds he was given.

FOXGLOVE
He loved trees so much that in all his journals, he mentioned only four flowers.

Washington was known as the "book farmer" because he first studied husbandry from British manuals and his keen interest led him to have more livestock than his peers. Today visitors see breeds that were available in the 18th century and similar to what Washington would have owned.

HOG ISLAND SHEEP
A rare breed named after an English settlement in Virginia; used for wool, food, mowing & fertilizer.

DOMINIQUE CHICKENS
Now a rare breed, these were once placed in coops with other chickens to pick bugs in the gardens.

DEER
Washington loved deer & created a deer park below the mansion along the Potomac River.

MULES
Probably the most prominent proponent of using mules in agriculture, Washington crossbred a male donkey from the King of Spain with a female horse.

AMERICAN SHAD
Alosa sapidissima

FISH
In spring slaves netted over a million shad and herring. The fish were salted, barreled & sold to markets along the coast as far as the West Indies.

At Mount Vernon, George Washington hired overseers for each of his farms, but he also found time to experiment with crop rotation, new types of farm buildings, and unique enterprises.

16-SIDED BARN Designed by Washington to more efficiently process wheat by enabling horses to tread wheat on the second floor

GRISTMILL. Built to increase production of flour and corn-meal, allowing Mount Vernon to export high-quality flour to the West Indies and Europe

THE GRISTMILL AND DISTILLERY COMPLEX HAD A COOPERAGE FOR MAKING BARRELS,

WHISKEY DISTILLERY One of Washington's most profitable ventures was suggested by his Scottish farm manager, who encouraged him to build a whiskey distillery next to the grist-mill. The distillery was the largest in America, and in 1799 produced 11,000 gallons of whiskey for a profit of $7,500—about $120,000 today.

THE HOMEY
COMFORT OF
POLITICS &
PROSE
BOOKSTORE

Appendix

Points of Interest in Washington DC and Surrounding Areas

African American Civil War
  Memorial Freedom Foundation
  and Museum
1200 U Street NW
(202) 667-2667
www.afroamcivilwar.org
Metro: U Street

Albert Einstein Memorial
National Academy of Sciences
  Building
Constitution Avenue and 22nd
  Street NW
www.nasonline.org

American University
4400 Massachusetts Avenue NW
(202) 885-1000
www.american.edu
Metro: Tenleytown/AU

Anacostia Riverwalk Trail
(202) 671-4678
www.ddot.dc.gov

Arena Stage
(In two venues until 2010 opening
  of Arena Stage at Mead Center
  for American Theater)
(202) 488-3300
www.arenastage.org

Arlington House (Robert E. Lee
  Memorial)
Arlington VA
(703) 235-1530
www.nps.gov/arho
Metro: Arlington National
  Cemetery

Arlington National Cemetery
Arlington VA
(703) 607-8000
www.arlingtoncemetery.org
Metro: Arlington National
Cemetery

Arthur M. Sackler Gallery
National Mall behind the
Smithsonian Castle
(202) 633-4880
www.asia.si.edu
Metro: Smithsonian

Bartholdi Park
Independence Avenue and 1st
Street SW
(202) 225-1116
www.usbg.gov/gardens/
barthodli-park.cfm
Metro: Federal Center SW

Bead Museum
400 7th Street NW
(202) 624-4500
www.beadmuseumdc.org
Metro: Gallery Place

Ben's Chili Bowl
1213 U Street NW
(202) 667-0909
www.benschilibowl.com
Metro: U Street

Bistro Bis
15 E Street NW
(202) 661-2700
www.bistrobis.com
Metro: Union Station

Blair House
1651–1653 Pennsylvania Avenue
NW
www.blairhouse.org
Metro: McPherson Square

Blues Alley
1073 Wisconsin Avenue NW
(202) 337-4141
www.bluesalley.com
Metro: Foggy Bottom

Bullfeathers of Capitol Hill
410 1st Street SE
(202) 488-2701
www.bullfeatherscapitolhill.com
Metro: Capitol South

Bureau of Engraving and Printing
14th and C Streets SW
(877) 874-4114
www.moneyfactory.gov
Metro: Smithsonian

Capitol Visitor Center
US Capitol
(202) 228-1793
www.aoc.gov/cvc/index.cfm
Metro: Capitol South

Captain White's Seafood City
1100 Maine Ave SW
(202) 484-2722
Metro: L'Enfant Plaza

Carlyle House Historic Park
121 N Fairfax Street
Alexandria VA
(703) 549-2997
www.carlylehouse.org
Metro: King Street

Catholic University of America
620 Michigan Avenue NE
(202) 319-5000
www.cua.edu
Metro: Brookland/CUA

Christ Church
118 N Washington Street
Alexandria VA
(703) 549-1450
www.historicchristchurch.org
Metro: King Street

Constitution Gardens
West Potomac Park
www.nps.gov/coga
Metro: Smithsonian

Corcoran College of Art and Design
500 17th Street NW
(202) 639-1801
www.corcoran.edu
Metro: Farragut West

Corcoran Gallery
500 17th Street NW
(202) 639-1700
www.corcoran.org
Metro: Farragut West

DAR
1776 D Street NW
(202) 628-1776
www.dar.org
Metro: Farragut West

DC Circulator
(202) 962-1423
www.dccirculator.com

DC Ducks
Union Station
(800) 213-2474
www.dcducks.com
Metro: Union Station

Dubliner
520 N Capitol Street NW
(202) 737-3773
www.dublinerdc.com
Metro: Union Station

Dumbarton House
2715 Q Street NW
(202) 337-2288
www.dumbartonhouse.org
Metro: Dupont Circle

Dumbarton Oaks
1703 32nd Street NW
(202) 339-6401
www.doaks.org
Metro: Dupont Circle

Eastern Market
225 7th Street SE
(202) 543-7293
www.easternmarketdc.com
Metro: Eastern Market

Embassy of the Republic of
   Indonesia
2020 Massachusetts Avenue NW
(202) 775-5200
www.embassyofindonesia.org
Metro: Dupont Circle

Filomena Ristorante
1063 Wisconsin Avenue NW
(202) 338-8800
www.filomena.com
Metro: Foggy Bottom

Folger Shakespeare Library
201 E Capitol Street SE
(202) 544-4600
www.folger.edu
Metro: Capitol South

Ford's Theatre National Historic
   Site
511 10th Street NW
(202) 426-6924
www.fordstheatre.org
Metro: Dupont Circle

Franklin Delano Roosevelt
   Memorial
Tidal Basin
www.nps.gov/fdrm

Frederick Douglass Museum
320 A Street NE
(202) 547-4273
www.nahc.org/fd/history.html
Metro: Union Station

Frederick Douglass National
   Historic Site
1411 W Street SE
(202) 426-5961
www.nps.gov/FRDO
Metro: Anacostia and B2 Bus

Freer Gallery of Art
National Mall at 12th Street SW
(202) 633-4880
www.asia.si.edu
Metro: Smithsonian

FRESHFARM Markets
(202) 362-8889
www.freshfarmmarket.org

Gadsby's Tavern Museum
134 N Royal Street
Alexandria VA
(703) 548-1288
www.gadsbystavernrestaurant
  .com
Metro: King Street

Gallaudet University
800 Florida Avenue NE
(202) 651-5000
www.gallaudet.edu
Metro: NY Ave/Florida Ave/
  Gallaudet U

George Washington University
2121 Eye Street NW
(202) 994-1000
www.gwu.edu
Metro: Foggy Bottom

Georgetown University
37th and O Streets NW
(202) 687-0100
www.georgetown.edu

Georgetown Waterfront Park
www.georgetownwaterfrontpark
  .org
Metro: McPherson Square

Harman Center for the Arts
www.shakespearetheatre.org
  Lansburgh Theatre
  450 7th Street NW
  (202) 547-1122
  Metro: Gallery Place/Chinatown

  Sidney Harman Hall
  610 F Street NW
  (202) 547-1122
  Metro: Gallery Place/Chinatown

The Hay-Adams
16th and H Streets NW
(202) 638-6600
www.hayadams.com
Metro: Metro Center

Hillwood Estate, Museum, and
  Gardens
4155 Linnean Avenue NW
(202) 686-5807
www.hillwoodmuseum.org
Metro: Van Ness/UDC

Howard University
2400 6th Street NW
(202) 806-6100
www.howard.edu
Metro: Shaw-Howard University

International Spy Museum
800 F Street NW
(202) EYESPYU
www.spymuseum.org
Metro: Gallery Place/Chinatown

Jack's Boathouse
3500 K Street NW
(202) 337-9642
www.jacksboathouse.com

Jefferson Memorial
W Potomac Park
www.nps.gov/thje/

Kennedy Center
(The John F. Kennedy Center for
   the Performing Arts)
2700 F Street NW
(800) 444-1324
www.kennedy-center.org
Metro: Foggy Bottom

Korean War Veterans Memorial
West Potomac Park
www.nps.gov/kwvm/

Kramerbooks and Afterwords
   Café and Grill
1517 Connecticut Ave NW
(202) 387-1400
www.kramers.com
Metro: Dupont Circle

Lafayette Square
www.lafayettesquare.org
Metro: McPherson Square

Library of Congress
101 Independence Avenue SE
(202) 707-5000
www.loc.gov
Metro: Capitol South

Lincoln Memorial
West Potomac Park
www.nps.gov/linc

Lunder Conservation Center
(see Smithsonian Donald W.
   Reynolds Center for American
   Art and Portraiture)

Lyceum
201 S Washington Street
Alexandria VA
(703) 838-4994
www.oha.alexandriava.gov/
   lyceum/
Metro: King Street

Madame Tussauds
1025 F Street NW
(888) WAX IN DC
www.madametussaudsdc.com
Metro: Metro Center

Madam's Organ
2461 18th Street NW
(202) 667-5370
www.madamsorgan.com
Metro: Woodley Park/Zoo/Adams
 Morgan

Maine Avenue Fish Market
1100 Maine Avenue SW
(202) 484-2722
Metro: L'Enfant Plaza

Maine Lobsterman
Washington Channel
Metro: Waterfront

Marian Koshland Science Museum
6th and E Streets NW
(202) 334-1201
www.koshland-science-museum
 .org
Metro: Gallery Place, Judiciary
 Square

Marine Corps War Memorial
Arlington Boulevard and Meade
 Street
Arlington VA
(703) 289-2500
www.nps.gov/archive/gwmp/
 usmc.htm
Metro: Rosslyn

Mansion on O Street
2020 O Street NW
(202) 496-2020
www.omansion.com
Metro: Dupont Circle

Mayflower Renaissance Hotel
1127 Connecticut Avenue NW
(202) 347-3000
www.marriott.com
Metro: Farragut West

Meridian Hill Park
Beginning at 16th and W Streets
 NW
(202) 895-6070
www.nps.gov/mehi
Metro: Columbia Heights

Metro (Washington Metropolitan
 Area Transit Authority)
(202) 962-1234
www.wmata.com

Michel Richard Citronelle
3000 M Street NW
(202) 625-2150
www.citronelledc.com
Metro: Foggy Bottom

Mie N Yu
3125 M Street NW
(202) 333-6122
www.mienyu.com
Metro: Foggy Bottom

Monocle Restaurant
107 D Street NE
(202) 546-4488
www.themonocle.com
Metro: Union Station

Montrose Park
30th and R Streets NW
(202) 895-6070
www.nps.gov/r0cr
Metro: Dupont Circle

Mount Vernon
3200 Mount Vernon Memorial
   Highway
Mount Vernon VA
(703) 780-2000
www.mountvernon.org
Metro: Huntington and Fairfax
   connector bus

Mount Zion Cemetery
27th and Q Streets NW
Metro: Dupont Circle

National Air and Space Museum
National Mall at 6th Street SW
(202) 633-1000
www.nasm.si.edu
Metro: L'Enfant Plaza

National Archives
Constitution Avenue at 7th Street
   NW
(866) 272-6272
www.archives.gov
Metro: Archives/Navy Memorial

National Building Museum
401 F Street NW
(202) 272-2448
www.nbm.org
Metro: Judiciary Square

National Cherry Blossom Festival
(877) 44BLOOM
www.nationalcherryblossom
   festival.org

National Gallery of Art
National Mall at 4th Street NW
(202) 737-4215
www.nga.gov
Metro: Judiciary Square

National Gallery of Art Sculpture
   Garden
National Mall at 7th Street NW
(202) 737-4215
www.nga.gov/feature/sculpture
   garden/
Metro: Archives

National Museum of African Art
National Mall behind the
  Smithsonian castle
(202) 633-4600
www.africa.si.edu
Metro: Smithsonian

National Museum of American
  History
National Mall at 14th Street NW
(202) 633-1000
www.americanhistory.si.edu
Metro: Federal Triangle

National Museum of Crime and
  Punishment
575 7th Street NW
(202) 393-1099
www.crimemuseum.org
Metro: Gallery Place/Chinatown

National Museum of Natural
  History
National Mall at 10th Street NW
(202) 633-1000
www.mnh.si.edu
Metro: Smithsonian

National Museum of the
  American Indian
National Mall at 4th Street SW
(202) 633-1000
www.americanindian.si.edu
Metro: L'Enfant Plaza

National Museum of Women in
  the Arts
1250 New York Avenue NW
(202) 783-5000
www.nmwa.org
Metro: Metro Center

National Portrait Gallery
8th and F Streets NW
(202) 633-8300
www.npg.si.edu
Metro: Gallery Place/Chinatown

National Postal Museum
2 Massachusetts Avenue NE
(202) 633-5555
www.postalmuseum.si.edu
Metro: Union Station

National Theatre
1321 Pennsylvania Avenue NW
(202) 628-6161
www.nationaltheatre.org
Metro: Metro Center

National Zoologoical Park
3001 Connecticut Avenue NW
(202) 633-4800
www.nationalzoo.si.edu
Metro: Woodley Park/Zoo

Nationals Park
1 Potomac Avenue SE
(202) 675-6287
www.mlb.mlb.com
Metro: Navy Yard

Newseum
555 Pennsylvania Avenue NW
(888) NEWSEUM
www.newseum.org
Metro: Archives

Oak Hill Cemetery
3001 R Street NW
(202) 337-2835
www.oakhillcemeterydc.org
Metro: Dupont Circle

Occidental Restaurant
1475 Pennsylvania Avenue NW
(202) 783-1475
www.occidentaldc.com
Metro: Metro Center

Old Ebbitt Grill
675 15th Street NW
(202) 347-4800
www.ebbitt.com
Metro: Metro Center

Old Post Office
1100 Pennsylvania Avenue NW
(202) 289-4224
www.oldpostofficedc.com
Metro: Federal Triangle

Old Stone House
3051 M Street NW
(202) 426-6851
www.nps.gov/olst/
Metro: Foggy Bottom

Oval Room
800 Connecticut Avenue NW
(202) 463-8700
www.ovalroom.com
Metro: Metro Center

Palm Restaurant
1225 19th Street NW
(202) 293-9091
www.thepalm.com
Metro: Dupont Circle

Peirce Mill
Rock Creek Park
(202) 895-6070
www.nps.gov/pimi

Pentagon Memorial
Army Navy Drive and Fern Street
Arlington VA
(202) 237-0327
www.pentagonmemorial.net
Metro: Pentagon

Phillips Colllection
1600 21st Street NW
(202) 387-2151
www.phillipscollection.org
Metro: Dupont Circle

Politics and Prose Bookstore
5015 Connecticut Avenue NW
(202) 364-1919
www.politics-prose.com
Metro: Van Ness/UDC

Robert F. Kennedy Memorial
  Stadium
Rock Creek Park
5200 Glover Road NW
(202) 895-6070
www.nps.gov/rocr

1789 Restaurant
1226 36th Street NW
(202) 965-1789
www.1789restaurant.com

Sewall-Belmont House
144 Constitution Avenue NE
(202) 546-1210
www.sewallbelmont.org
Metro: Union Station

Shakepeare Theatre Company
(see Harman Center for the Arts)

Smithsonian American Art
  Museum's Luce Foundation
  Center for American Art
(see Smithsonian Donald W.
  Reynolds Center for American
  Art and Portraiture)

Smithsonian American Art
  Museum's Renwick Gallery
Pennsylvania Avenue at 17th
  Street NW
(202) 633-1000
www.americanart.si.edu
Metro: Farragut West

Smithsonian Castle
(Smithsonian Information Center)
National Mall SW
(202) 633-1000
www.si.edu
Metro: Smithsonian

Smithsonian Donald W. Reynolds
  Center for American Art and
  Portraiture
Smithsonian American Art
  Museum and the National
  Portrait Gallery
8th and F Streets NW
(202) 633-1000
www.americanart.si.edu
Metro: Gallery Place/Chinatown

Smithsonian Hirshhorn Museum
  and Sculpture Garden
National Mall at 7th Street SW
(202) 633-4674
www.hirshhorn.si.edu
Metro: L'Enfant Plaza

Southeastern University
501 I Street SW
(202) 478-8200
www.seu.edu
Metro: Waterfront

Stabler-Leadbeater Apothecary
  Museum
105–107 S Fairfax Street
Alexandria VA
(703) 838-3852
www.apothecarymuseum.org
Metro: King Street

Stephen Decatur House Museum
1610 H Street NW
(202) 842-0920
www.decaturhouse.org
Metro: Farragut West

St. John's Episcopal Church
1525 H Street NW
(202) 347-8766
www.stjohns-dc.org
Metro: McPherson Square

Studio Theatre
1501 14th Street NW
(202) 332-3300
www.studiotheatre.org
Metro: Dupont Circle

Tabard Inn
1739 N Street NW
(202) 785-1277
www.tabardinn.com
Metro: Dupont Circle

Textile Museum
2320 S Street NW
(202) 667-0441
www.textilemuseum.org
Metro: Dupont Circle

Theodore Roosevelt Island
  Memorial
George Washington Memorial
  Parkway
www.nps.gov/this
Metro: Rosslyn

Torpedo Factory Art Center
105 N Union Street
Alexandria VA
(703) 838-4565
www.torpedofactory.org
Metro: King Street

Tryst Coffeehouse and Bar
2459 18th Street NW
(202) 232-5500
www.trystdc.com
Metro: Woodley Park/Zoo/Adams
  Morgan

Tudor Place Historic House and
  Garden
1644 31st Street NW
(202) 965-0400
www.tudorplace.org
Metro: Dupont Circle

Twilight Tattoo
(202) 685-2888
www.mdw.army.mil/tlt/

Union Station
49 Massachusetts Avenue SE
www.unionstationdc.com
(202) 289-1908
Metro: Union Station

United States Air Force Memorial
1 Air Force Memorial Drive
Arlington VA
(703) 979-0674
www.airforcememorial.org
Metro: Pentagon

United States Botanic Garden
100 Maryland Avenue SW
(202) 225-8333
www.usbg.gov
Metro: Federal Center SW

United States Capitol
www.aoc.gov
Metro: Capitol South

United States Holocaust
  Memorial Museum
100 Raoul Wallenberg Place SW
(202) 488-0400
www.ushmm.org
Metro: Smithsonian

United States Navy Memorial
701 Pennsylvania Avenue NW
(202) 737-2300
www.navymemorial.org
Metro: Archives

United States Supreme Court
1 1st Street NE
(202) 479-3030
www.supremecourtus.gov
Metro: Capitol South

University of the District of
  Columbia
4200 Connecticut Avenue NW
(202) 274-5000
www.udc.edu
Metro: Van Ness/UDC

Verizon Center
601 F Street NW
(202) 661-5000
www.verizoncenter.com
Metro: Gallery Place/Chinatown

Vietnam Veterans Memorial
West Potomac Park
www.nps.gov/vive/

Warner Theatre
1299 Pennsylvania Avenue NW
(202) 783-4000
www.warnertheatre.com
Metro: Metro Center

Washington Monument
West Potomac Park
www.nps.gov/wamo
Metro: Smithsonian

Washington National Cathedral
3101 Wisconsin Avenue NW
(202) 537-6200
www.nationalcathedral.org
Metro: Tenleytown/AU

White House
1600 Pennsylvania Avenue NW
www.whitehouse.gov
Metro: Metro Center

White House Visitor Center
SE corner of 15th and E Streets
(202) 456-7041
www.whitehouse.gov/history/
    tours/
Metro: Federal Triangle

Willard InterContinental
    Washington
1401 Pennsylvania Avenue NW
(202) 628-9100
www.washington.inter
    continental.com
Metro: Metro Center

Women's *Titanic* Memorial
Washington Channel at P Street
    SW
www.titanic-titanic.com
Metro: Waterfront

Woodrow Wilson House
2340 S Street NW
(202) 387-4062
www.woodrowwilsonhouse.org
Metro: Dupont Circle

Woolly Mammoth Theater
641 D Street NW
(202) 289-2443
www.woollymammoth.net
Metro: Archives

World War II Memorial
West Potomac Park at 17th Street
    NW
(202) 619-7222
www.nps.gov/nwwm

Zed's Ehtiopian Cuisine
1201 28th Street NW
202-333-4710
www.zeds.net
Metro: Foggy Bottom

Acknowledgments

Thank you and farewell to my talented editor of nine years, Antonia Fusco, who is admirably following her new dream.

Thank you to true friends like Alyse O'Neill for putting me in touch with DC authors Cheryl and Peter Barnes and Randall and Tom Phillips; Patsy Graham for introducing me to Honey Alexander; Jacke McCurdy for helping me in a pinch; and Mary Tufty Meek for compiling a daunting "DC to do" list that served as a personal challenge.

High praise to everyone "inside the beltway" who came to my aid; you showed pride in your jobs and were eager to help. I am especially grateful to Marv Solberg, Glenn DeMarr, and Kathy Langley who made an extra effort to share their passion for DC history; Rebecca Pawlowski of the Washington DC Convention and Tourism Corporation who answered my questions for a year; and Elaine S. Patterson and Lisa McGovern for being my go-to girls for local knowledge.

LEARNING FROM THE MASTERS AT THE NATIONAL GALLERY OF ART.

Thank you to those who helped make this book possible: Sakura of America, whose art products are used for the illustrations; Orlando Adiao, who has cleverly designed my covers; and Algonquin's Andra Olenik and Lindsay Olson, who have the most satisfying job of finally putting this baby to bed.

My loving gratitude to Eric and Shirley Gessler for being part of our DC adventure and to the rest of our family and friends, I love you all for celebrating even the book's smallest milestones with me. To my husband, Paul, who has been so very patient, loving, and sacrificing, you are truly my Mr. Wonderful.

Credits

Pages vi and 6: 1793 Map from the Library of Congress

Page 29: Building reference photo courtesy Marv Solberg, dcMemorials.com

Page 32: *The Four Gospels* (Codex Washingtonensis). Late 4th to early 5th century, ink on parchment. Origin: Egypt. *Harmony in Blue and Gold: The Peacock Room,* 1876-1877. James McNeill Whistler, oil paint and gold leaf on canvas, leather, and wood.

Page 42: *Typewriter Eraser, Scale X,* by Claes Oldenburg and Coosje van Bruggen. Gift of the Morris and Gwendolyn Cafritz Foundation. Courtesy the Oldenburg van Bruggen Foundation. © 2008 Claes Oldenburg and Coosje van Bruggen. *An Entrance to the Paris Métropolitain,* Hector Guimard. Gift of Robert P. and Arlene R. Kogod.

Page 49: *Vietnam Women's Memorial.* © 1993, Vietnam Women's Memorial Foundation, Inc. Glenna Goodacre, sculptor.

Page 108: *The Spirit of Freedom* sculpture by Ed Hamilton

Page 120: *Space Window,* by Rodney Winfield. Reference photos courtesy Marv Solberg, dcMemorials.com. *Alligator,* designed by Carl Tucker and carved by Edward Ratti. *Darth Vader,* winning design by Chris Rader was carved by Patrick Plunkett from a model by Jay Carpenter.

Page 122: Teapot: Alexandria Archaeology Museum, City of Alexandria VA

RISTORANTE
PICCOLO
A ROMANTIC
ITALIAN
TRATTORIA

Index

Bistro Bis, 82
Blair House, 74
Bleifeld, Stanley, 63
Bliss, Mildred, 104
Bliss, Robert Woods, 104
Blues Alley, 102
Booth, John Wilkes, 90
Botanic Garden, United States, 22
Braddock, General, 128
Brady, Mathew, 51
Brumidi, Constantino, 9
Bullfeathers of Capitol Hill, 82
Bunshaft, Gordon, 29
Bureau of Engraving and Printing, 36
Burnham, Daniel, 18
Burns, Lucy, 17
Bush, Barbara, 70, 73
Bush, Laura, 70
bus service, 15

Canal Company, 95
C & O Canal, 100
Capitol, the, 6, 8–9
    grounds, 10–11
    Visitor Center, 1, 8
Capitol Hill, 1–25
    Historic District, 20
Carle, Dorothy Henrietta Scharff, 64
Carlyle, George, 128
Carlyle, John, 128
Carlyle House Historic Park, 128
Carroll, John, 98
Carter, Rosalynn, 70

Catholic University of America, 98
cemeteries, 105
    Arlington National Cemetery, 5, 60, 61
Central Park, New York City, 10
Chambers, Whitaker, 88
cherry blossoms, 53, 54–55
chess in Dupont Circle, 107
Chew, Cassandra, 96
Chicago American History Museum, 91
Chinatown, 63, 92
Chinese Imperial Commission, 28
Christ Church, 124
Christmas Tree on the Ellipse, National, 72
City Beautiful movement, 18, 25
Clay, Henry, 67
Clinton, Hillary, 70, 73
Columbus, Christopher, 4
Constitution, US, 78
Constitution Avenue, 78–79
Constitution Gardens, 48
copyright law, 14
Corcoran, William Wilson, 65, 66, 105
Corcoran College of Art and Design, 98
Corcoran Gallery of Art, 65
Crime and Punishment, National Museum of, 83
Curtius, Dr. Philippe, 89
Custis, George Washington Parke, 60
Custis, Martha, 103

Rock Creek Park, 111, 117
Roosevelt, Edith, 72
Roosevelt, Eleanor, 70
Roosevelt, Franklin D., 56, 73
Roosevelt, Theodore, 58, 68, 71, 73
Root, Elihu, 5
Rose Garden, 72
Ruth, Babe, 37

Sackler, Dr. Arthur M., 33
Safford, Henry, 91
St. John's Church, 74
Sakura Matsuri Japanese street festival, 55
Scidmore, Eliza Ruhamah, 54
Science Museum, 81
Seal of the United States, 79
1789 Restaurant, 102
Sewall-Belmont House, 17
Shakespeare, William, 13
Shaw, Colonel Robert, 108
Shaw neighborhood, 108–10
Sheridan-Kalorama Historic District, 114–15
Smithson, James, 30
Smithsonian American Art Museum, 86–87
Smithsonian Castle, 66
Smithsonian Information Center, 30
Smithsonian Institution, 39
  gardens, 41
  museums, 19, 26, 28–34, 37, 40–41, 66, 86–87

Smithsonian Institution Building, 30
Smithsonian National Zoo, 118
Sousa, John Philip, 47
Southeastern University, 98
South Korea, 52
Spencer, Lilly Martin, 93
Spirit of Freedom Memorial, 108
Stabler, Edward, 125
Stabler-Leadbeater Apothecary Museum, 125
stadiums, 84–85
Star-Spangled Banner, 38
State Department, 79
Stephen Decatur House Museum, 74
Steven F. Udvar-Hazy Center, 28
Stuart, Gilbert, 86
Studio Theatre, 80
Supreme Court, 12

Tabard Inn, 107
Taft, Helen, 54, 70
Taft, William Howard, 71, 73
Ten Bells of Congress, 76
Textile Museum, 114
theaters, 80
Theodore Roosevelt Island, 58
Theodore Roosevelt Island National Memorial, 58
Thornton, William, 9
Three Soldiers, 49
Tidal Basin, 53
Titanic, 121
Tomb of the Unknowns, 61

Lucky
in
Left Field

Lucky
in
Left Field

BETSY DUFFEY
illustrated by Leslie Morrill

SIMON & SCHUSTER BOOKS FOR YOUNG READERS
Published by Simon & Schuster
New York   London   Toronto   Sydney   Tokyo   Singapore

SIMON & SCHUSTER BOOKS FOR YOUNG READERS
Simon & Schuster Building
Rockefeller Center
1230 Avenue of the Americas
New York, New York 10020
SIMON & SCHUSTER BOOKS FOR YOUNG READERS
is a trademark of Simon & Schuster.
Designed by Vicki Kalajian
Manufactured in the United States of America

10 9 8 7 6 5 4 3 2 1

Library of Congress Cataloging-in-Publication Data
Duffey, Betsy. Lucky in left field / by Betsy Duffey;
illustrated by Leslie Morrill.   p.   cm.
Summary: Lucky the dog tries to regain his spot as left fielder
on his master's losing baseball team after a new coach
arrives and banishes Lucky from the ball park.
[1. Dogs—Fiction.   2. Baseball—Fiction.]   I. Morrill, Leslie H., ill.
II. Title. PZ7.D876Lu   1992 [Fic]—dc20   91–45791 CIP
ISBN: 0-671-74687-1

Contents

A Dog in the Outfield

"ERF! ERF!"

Lucky barked his encouragement from the outfield. He danced back and forth, ready to catch any balls that came his way. Lucky played left field for the Expos.

"ERF! ERF!"

The Expos needed all the encouragement they could get. They had never won a game.

George played third base. He shuffled his feet. He looked back at Lucky and smiled. His dog was one of the best players on the team.

The Giants were at bat. They were undefeated.

1

The Expos were ready. Mike at first. Kritter at second. Jill at short stop. Jay pitching. Steve catching. Right field, Millie. Center field, Tripp. And in left field, Lucky.

George's friend Bart had played left field for the first half of the season, until he moved to Alabama. Then the Expos had been short one player.

They played one game without a left fielder. Halfway through the game Lucky ran out onto the field to stop a grounder. He ran with it to George as fast as he could. George threw the batter out at first.

Ever since that day Lucky had been on the team.

Chipper Davis came up to the plate to bat for the Giants. He swung the bat a few times to warm up.

"ERF! ERF!"

George waved his glove as a signal for Lucky to be quiet. All the Expos were silent. They watched Jay give the pitch.

Chipper swung and . . .

2

"ERF! ERF!"

Chipper missed! Strike one!

"Quiet, Lucky!" George signaled with his glove again.

Jay wound up and gave the second pitch.

"ERF! ERF!"

Chipper missed again! Strike two!

Chipper's face was red. He looked at Lucky sitting in the outfield and put his hands on his hips. He gritted his teeth.

George signaled again for Lucky to be quiet.

Jay pitched.

"ERF! ERF!"

Crack! This time Chipper did not miss.

The ball soared high in the air. Up over the pitcher's head, over second base, over center field, and over the tall grass behind center field.

When balls went into the grass behind center field, only Lucky could find them. He ran after the flying ball. He was a streak. A streak of moving legs and flapping ears.

Even Lucky could not get the ball this time. The ball flew over the tall grass and over the white fence at the back of the field. The ball was history.

Chipper ran the bases in a slow jog.

"Thanks, Lucky!" Chipper called out as he passed between second and third base.

Lucky wagged his tail and headed back to left field.

"Home run!" the umpire called out.

George groaned. The Giants had won the game.

The Expos lined up on one side of the field and the Giants lined up on the other side of the field. The two lines passed each other.

George shook hands with each of the Giants as they passed him. Lucky waited at the end of the line. The Giants patted him on the head as they passed.

George picked up his glove and called Lucky with a whistle.

Ten games, ten losses. George walked with

his head low, Lucky next to him. It sure would be nice to win for once.

"Hey, George," Kritter called, "don't forget practice tomorrow." He smiled at George and gave the thumbs-up sign.

George smiled at Kritter and returned the sign.

Tomorrow there would be new hope for the Expos. Jay's older brother, Chet, was coming home from college. Chet played on a college team. He was a great baseball player.

Last summer Jay's parents had taken George and the whole Expos team to see Chet play. Chet had played like a pro. He hit one double, one triple, and one fantastic home run to tie the game. He had been a hero that day.

Chet was terrific. And the most terrific part was that Chet was going to be coaching the Expos while he was home for the summer. The Expos had never had a real coach before.

Things would be different with a coach

like Chet. The Expos might finally win a game. After ten losses they really needed a win.

George smiled at Lucky.

With Chet as their coach the ten-game losing streak would finally end.

"We're going to be great!" he said. Lucky barked twice in agreement.

Summer Schedules

Lucky walked along happily beside George. Winning or losing made no difference to Lucky.

Lucky loved summer. Lucky loved baseball.

Summer days stretched out before him one after another. Now it was just about 3:15 in the afternoon. Time for him to chase the tabby cat next door.

He had his summer all planned out. His morning schedule went like this:

7:00. Wake up in kitchen. (He had trained his people not to make him sleep in the doghouse.) Sniff kitchen floor for crumbs.

7:05. Run upstairs. Jump on the boy. Lick him until his eyes open.

7:10. Let the boy fix breakfast. Beg for scraps of bacon or sausage.

7:15. Bark at the door. He had trained the boy to open the door when he barked. Go outside. Sniff. Circle three times. Make a puddle. His people got very upset if he left the going-outside part out of his schedule.

8:00. Check backyard. Mark territory. Sniff carefully all corners.

9:00. Dig around under the pecan tree. Chew on bones if found.

9:15. Go back inside and lie down in front of refrigerator again. Nap till lunch.

Sometimes the boy would take him along for a ride in the backseat of the car or walk him around the block.

What terrific mornings he had! The only thing better than Lucky's summer mornings were Lucky's summer afternoons. Every afternoon since school was out, the boy had taken him to play BASEBALL.

Baseball was wonderful! A whole bunch of kids got together. They threw balls to each other. They got very excited, ran in circles, and hit the balls with sticks.

It was great. Running and throwing balls and yelling and sticks and kids. All the things that dogs love the most.

Best of all they let Lucky play with them.

Dog heaven!

Lucky had learned two new words this summer. The happiest words that he had learned yet in his life: PLAY BALL!

They were almost home. Lucky wagged his tail as he thought about the tabby cat.

His thoughts were interrupted by a yell. One of the other boys ran up to them. He was excited. Lucky could tell by the way his voice sounded. Lucky began to thump his tail. He loved excitement!

What were they saying? He cocked his head to the right and listened. Maybe they would say some words that he knew.

"Baseball." He knew that one. It was a

good word. He thumped his tail harder. *Thump. Thump.*

"Practice." That was a good word. *Thump. Thump.*

"Now!" Lucky knew what that meant.

He had heard that word a lot from his people. They said things like:

"Lucky put down that shoe *now*!" or

"Lucky get down from the sofa *now*!"

"Now" meant that something was about to happen fast. In the case of the sofa or the shoe, it usually meant a whack on the behind. Today it must mean a *baseball practice* was about to start right away.

The boys began to run back toward the ball field.

Lucky couldn't believe his luck. They were going to play baseball twice in one day!

He ran down the street with the boys.

His afternoon schedule had just changed for the better. That pesky cat would just have to wait.

Coach Chet

Chet was in town a day early. The Expos had a coach.

George and Lucky ran back down the street. Chet was going to meet them at the ball field for a practice. Kritter had told George.

George remembered Chet playing at the university game. The Yankees had been behind 7 to 4. He would never forget the last inning. Chet came up to bat. There was a runner on first and a runner on second. There were two outs.

The crowd went wild. Chet was the best hitter on the Yankees. If Chet could hit the

two runners home and score himself, the game would be tied.

He warmed up. The crowd began a chant.

"CHET! CHET! CHET! CHET!"

He swung. He connected. He took off. George could still see the ball soaring through the air like slow motion over the heads of the players.

He could still remember the crowds of people jumping up and down in the stands.

He could still remember Chet running the bases, waving to the crowds. He had tied the game.

George could still remember what he had thought as he watched Chet running the bases.

I want to be just like Chet!

Now he had his chance. The day seemed brighter. George ran to the ball field with his head high. He could hardly wait for practice to start.

When he got to the field he could see a

red sports car parked at the curb. It was shiny and polished. It must belong to Chet. He couldn't believe that Chet was really going to be their coach.

Side by side, George and Lucky ran onto the field. George could see Chet now. He was swinging a bat to warm up.

He had on a real baseball uniform. White baseball pants with a light-blue jersey. Number five was on the back of the jersey. Some of the kids were already at the ball field and they clustered around Chet, watching every swing.

George ran faster. He was eager to practice, eager to learn what Chet could teach him.

Halfway across the field, Coach Chet looked up at George and Lucky. George smiled his biggest smile and waved at Chet.

Chet did not wave back. He kept swinging the bat and watching George and Lucky run toward him.

From across the field George could see

him frown. What was wrong? George didn't want to do something wrong at the very first practice.

Was it the way he was running? Had he forgotten something? He looked down to be sure he had his glove.

Yes, he had his glove. What else could it be?

As they ran up to the group, Coach Chet spat on the ground and pointed at Lucky. "Why did you bring the dog?" he asked George.

George stopped short. Had he heard Chet right? He looked down at Lucky. Lucky's tail was wagging.

"Lucky plays left field," George said.

Coach Chet laughed. "Now I've heard everything," he said. "A dog on a baseball team." He shook his head. "The dog has got to go."

The Expos gathered around Chet. "No," they all said together.

Mike patted Lucky on the head. "We *need* Lucky," he said.

"Lucky is a great left fielder," said Jay.

"We can't play without Lucky," said Jill.

Coach Chet shook his head again. He reached down and picked Lucky up. Lucky licked his face. "George," he said, "you have a great little dog here. But that's all he is. A dog, not a baseball player."

He put Lucky down beside George. Lucky wagged his tail.

George looked at Lucky then back at Coach Chet.

"But—" he said.

Coach Chet held up his hand and continued. "A dog on the field is dangerous. Dogs can trip the runner. They interfere with the play of the game. You can't play good baseball if you are worried about stepping on a dog on the field."

"But—" George said again.

"Baseballs are hard," Coach Chet went on. "Players have to watch out for the ball all the time. A little dog like that could get hurt by a ball."

"But"—George started again—"we can't win without Lucky," he said. The other team members nodded their heads.

Chet looked around at each kid. "Have you been winning *with* Lucky?" he asked.

The kids shook their heads.

"Well?"

George looked at Chet. He looked at the other Expos. No one said anything.

"Well," Chet asked again, "who wants to win?"

Everyone nodded.

"Okay," said Chet. "Tripp, you cover left." He reached down and gave Lucky one more rub on the head. Then he looked up at George and his face went from a smile to a serious look.

"You can put him in the storage shed today." He pointed to the small shed where the equipment was kept. "Then tomorrow, leave the mutt at home."

Mutt

MUTT!

Lucky stopped wagging his tail.

Lucky knew the name *mutt*!

It was not a good name.

His mother had told him all about dog names before he had been adopted.

When you heard the good names everything was okay. People who liked you used the good names. Some good names were *good boy, fellah, pooch, honey, darlin'*.

Bad names were a different story.

When you heard the bad names, it meant *look out*. People who did not like you used

the bad names. Sometimes when they used the bad names, they kicked you.

Some bad names were *bad boy, jerk, bat breath, flea bag,* and *mutt.*

Mutt was one of the worst of the bad names. And this big boy, this man was calling him *mutt.*

His boy would defend him.

The nerve! Calling him a *mutt*!

The boy would set the man straight.

Lucky stood a little closer to the boy. He got behind the boy's legs and peered out at the man. He waited for the boy to defend him.

But the boy was quiet.

The man was pointing toward the storage shed where they kept the bats and balls when they were not playing.

Lucky had a bad feeling about the way the man looked at the storage shed. He was glad he was with the boy.

When he was with the boy, he could be

sure that nothing bad would happen to him. He could always trust the boy.

The boy took his collar and began to pull him toward the shed.

Lucky rolled his eyes at the shed.

He could trust the boy, he told himself. The boy *would* defend him. He just knew it.

So why was the boy pulling him toward the shed now? He began to tremble.

The boy wouldn't let him down.

He looked up at the boy and gave him his most appealing look. His "I am pitiful" look. A look that he had learned from his mother, who had learned it from a golden retriever. For this look he lowered his head and rolled his eyes up at George. It was a look that couldn't be resisted—he hoped.

He dug his feet into the ground and straightened his legs. The boy only pulled him harder.

The door opened.

He could trust the boy—couldn't he?

The boy pushed him into the shed.

The door of the storage shed slammed shut.

Bang!

It was the saddest sound that Lucky had ever heard.

But then, locked in the storage shed he heard something even sadder.

The two happiest words that he knew became the two saddest words that he knew.

"PLAY BALL!"

The practice had started without him.

Hustle! Hustle!

AAAAOOOOO!

George tried to ignore the wail coming from the storage shed but it was impossible.

He thought about how Lucky had looked at him when he closed the door to the shed. It had been a pitiful look, a look that made George feel bad all the way through.

He hoped that Chet knew what he was doing. Chet had ten years of experience. He knew everything there was to know about baseball. George put his hands on his knees and got ready to catch any balls that Chet hit his way.

"Let's go, kids!" called Chet. "Hustle, hustle."

Chet put all the team in the outfield and started hitting balls to them. He threw the balls up one at a time and hit them with the bat.

"Now get it!" he called out. "Hustle!"

Crack!

The first ball soared over left field into the tall grass.

Crack!

The second ball soared over center field into the tall grass.

Crack!

The third ball soared over left field into the tall grass.

The kids scrambled to look for the lost balls in the grass. Without Lucky they would have to find them themselves. Balls were valuable and they didn't want to lose any. Most of all they didn't want to let Chet down.

"Tighten it up out there, you guys," Chet

called out. "Get under the ball. Trap the ball in the pocket of your glove."

Crack! Chet hit more balls to the team.

Kritter got under one. He trapped it in the pocket of his glove.

"Way to go!" called Chet.

Crack! Chet hit another one.

The ball soared. It was a high pop fly right to George. George got his glove ready. He got under the ball.

AAAAOOOOO!

He tried to concentrate. He tried not to think about Lucky in the storage shed. He wanted to show Chet what a good catcher he was. He reached out his glove for the ball. He missed.

The ball bounced back into the grass.

Chet groaned. George scrambled to find the ball.

"HUSTLE! HUSTLE!" yelled Chet.

AAAOOOO!

For the first time George wanted practice

to be over. For the first time baseball was not fun.

ERF! ERF! ERRRF!

What was so terrible about a dog on the team anyway? George sighed. He turned and threw the ball back to Chet. He tried not to think about Lucky.

George put this hands on his knees and got ready for the next ball. Was this what it took to be a good baseball player? Chet was the best. If this was what it took, he would try it.

He pounded his fist in his glove a few times and watched Chet get ready to hit another one.

AAAOOOO!

It was going to be a long afternoon.

The Misery Howl

It was a long afternoon for Lucky too.

AAAAOOOOO!

He called out for George.

From inside the storage shed he could hear the crack of the bat hitting the balls. In his mind he could imagine the balls soaring higher, higher over left field and he was not there to catch them.

AAAAOOOOO!

He couldn't bear the thought. They were playing baseball without him.

He scratched at the old wooden door of the storage shed. He was desperate.

Crack!

He heard the bat again. They needed him. They needed him in left field.

AAAAAOOOOOO!

The boy had to hear him. If the boy heard him, surely he would come and let him out.

Lucky tried to remember what his mother had taught him about barking.

There were many different kinds of dog barks. Each had its special use.

The Broken Record Bark:

You bark over and over like a broken record. ERF! ERF!, ERF! ERF!, ERF! ERF!, ERF! ERF!

It tortures the people into giving you what you want. It works best at night. He had used it to teach the boy to sleep with him in the doghouse.

It would not work now.

The Chain Letter Bark:

When you hear another dog bark in the neighborhood, you have to bark back. Then the dog in the next house must bark to pass it on.

It would not work now.

The Demand Bark:

This bark is one short *ERF!* used to indicate to your people that you want something.

When you bark at the door, they open it.

When you bark at the refrigerator, they feed you.

When you bark at your water bowl, they fill it up.

It would not work now.

The Misery Howl:

A howl for times of deepest despair. It is not a howl that you mean to use or even plan to use. It is a howl that comes out in times of pure misery.

Lucky used it now.

AAAAAAAAAOOOOOOOOOOO!

It was a time of deep despair.

Chewing Tobacco

Chet called the team in from the field.

He spit brown liquid onto the grass and began to talk about fielding.

"Whenever I nod my head, the play is at first. The batter hits, we get the ball and throw him out at first. Let's try it."

"Now, watch my head," he said. He nodded his head up and down. "Now, where's the play?"

"At first," the kids answered.

Chet spit again.

"Let's try it!" he said. The team ran back to their positions.

Chet began to hit grounders to the team.

Before each hit he nodded his head. The Expos chased each grounder and threw them to Mike on first. As Mike caught each one, Chet would yell *"Out!"*

After he had hit ten balls, he called them back for a pep talk.

George and Jill ran in together.

"He's great!" Jill said. George nodded his agreement. They were already learning from Chet.

Chet motioned for them to come closer.

"You gotta hustle! You gotta go after the ball. Now we're gonna have a little batting practice. I'll pitch and you show me whatcha got."

He spit again.

George wondered what was in Chet's mouth. Chet took a red-and-white packet from his back pocket and unrolled the top.

All the Expos went closer to see.

"What's that?" Jill asked.

Chet pushed them back.

"Chewing tobacco," he said. He nudged

Jay with his elbow and laughed. "You can't play baseball without chewing tobacco!"

He held the open packet out to the kids. "Here, try it. It'll make a ball player out of you."

George peered into the envelope. Inside was something brown and crinkly. It didn't smell good. He didn't like the look of the chewing tobacco and he didn't like the brown liquid that Chet was spitting out.

Jill stepped back.

"Yuck!" she said. "I don't want any."

Chet pulled the envelope back. "You guys are wimps," he said. "All the pros chew tobacco."

"Here, Jay," said Chet. He slapped Jay on the back. "You want some, don't you? Help yourself."

Jay looked at the packet for a moment. Then he reached in and pulled out a bit of the stringy brown tobacco. He looked at it closely and then stuffed it into his pocket. "For later," he said to Chet.

"Anyone else?" Chet asked. He passed the packet around the circle in front of each player.

No one moved.

When it passed Jill, she wrinkled her nose.

No one else reached into the bag.

"Last chance," said Chet.

No one moved.

"Then let's play some ball!"

Chet rolled up the package and pushed it to George.

"Here, buddy, have the rest." He put the packet in George's hand. "Now," he said to George, "you bat." Chet turned and walked back to the pitcher's mound.

George looked at the bag in his hand. His face felt red. He stuck it into his back pocket and picked up the bat.

He didn't want the tobacco but he didn't know how to give it back. He could think about it later. He moved to the plate.

Chet wound up his arm to pitch to

George. From the pitcher's mound he watched George holding the bat.

"Choke up!" he called out. "Choke up!"

Chet pitched a fast ball. George swung and missed.

"*Choke up!*" Chet called again. "Get the bat off your shoulder."

George swung again. This time he hit the ball. The ball rolled between first and second base and stopped.

Not a good hit.

"Okay!" Chet called out. "Try to get the bat around a little faster."

He pitched again.

George swung again. Faster this time. This time he didn't miss.

Crack!

This time he hit a line drive right down the third base line.

Perfect! It was his best hit ever.

George looked at Chet. Chet was grinning.

"That's it!" Chet said. "You just listen to me and you'll be great!"

George smiled. He got ready for the next pitch.

He choked up on the bat. He held it up off his shoulder. He got ready to get it around faster.

Chet knew a lot about baseball. He would listen to Chet.

Chet spit again and wound up to throw the next pitch.

"Think only of the ball," he said.

George tried to think only of the ball. He had a hard time. He kept thinking of Lucky in the shed. Lucky hadn't barked in a while. Was he okay?

He kept thinking of the chewing tobacco. The bulge of the package in his back pocket felt tight. He kept thinking about Chet's words:

"It'll make a ball player out of you."

Paw over Paw

Lucky scratched some more at the old wooden door of the storage shed. The barking had not worked. He needed another plan.

The floor of the shed was dirt. Lucky began to scratch under the door using his best digging motion. One paw over the other, over and over. Maybe he could dig a hole big enough to climb out.

It was hot in the shed. He was panting now.

He had to get out. The kids were playing baseball without him.

He stopped digging and tried out his hole.

He poked his nose into the hole as far as it would go. Just under the door his nose came out on the other side.

Sniff.

He got a whiff of fresh air.

Sniff.

He sniffed again.

Now he could smell the smells of the ball field, *baseball* smells.

It smelled like a mixture of popcorn, leather, sweat, boys and girls, and best of all *his* boy. He pulled his nose back into the shed and began to dig some more.

Paw over paw.

The hole was getting bigger and bigger.

Crack! He heard a bat hit a ball again.

Center field. He could tell by the sound of it. He imagined the ball sailing through the air. The next one might come to left field, his position.

He had to get out.

The team needed him.

He began to dig faster.

Paw over paw.

He tried out the hole again. He could get his whole head through. He dug harder.

Paw over paw over paw over paw.

His front paws fit.

Paw over paw. Was the hole big enough now?

He wriggled his whole body into the hole and for a moment he was stuck. Panic!

He had not done all that hard work just to end up stuck in his hole!

He began to wiggle back and forth in the hole. While he wiggled, he scraped the dirt in front of him and pulled himself forward. Then with a groan, he gave an extra push and wriggled all the way out.

He rolled on his back in the grass beside the field. His body and paws were covered with the red dirt.

The air had never smelled so fresh and sweet. It felt wonderful on his face.

The grass had never felt so soft and good.

He rubbed his back on the grass, wiggling back and forth.

Crack!

The game!

In his excitement at getting out of the storage shed, he had almost forgotten the game!

He rolled over onto his feet and ran happily toward left field. He had to get the ball.

This time he would not take the ball to the boy. If Lucky took the ball to the boy, he might end up back in the shed.

Up ahead he saw the ball drop into left field. Now it was time to play a different game. The one that the boy called Keep Away.

Keep Away

"I told you to keep the mutt off the field."
Chet threw his glove down.

George watched Lucky running across left field. Lucky grabbed the baseball and began to run around the field.

George dropped his bat and began to chase him. One by one the other kids joined in the chase.

Lucky lay down in the grass and rolled his eyes up at George, waiting. He held the ball in his mouth. His tail thumped on the grass.

Thump. Thump. He waited, tense and ready. When George was almost close enough to grab him, he darted away, run-

ning at top speed to another part of the field. Then he lay down again until someone else got close.

Thump. Thump.

Lucky loved a good game of Keep Away.

George began to laugh. Jay began to laugh, then Kritter and Jill. The whole team was laughing and chasing Lucky.

The baseball game had become a game of Keep Away.

The only one not laughing was Coach Chet. The baseball practice was forgotten.

"What kind of team is this anyway?" Chet called out.

No one heard him. They were too busy chasing Lucky all over the baseball field.

Tweeet! Chet blew a sharp blast on the whistle around his neck. The kids stopped laughing and running and looked at Chet.

Chet put his hands on his hips. His face was hardened into a serious frown.

Thump. Thump.

Lucky sat, staring at Chet. George saw his

chance to get the ball back while Lucky was off guard. He grabbed for him. Lucky was too fast and George hit the dirt in a belly smacker. Lucky stopped just out of reach and thumped his tail again.

The other players roared with laughter.

George looked back at Chet.

Chet was shaking his head. Would Chet throw him off the team?

Then Chet's frown broke and he joined the laughter. He waved his glove at them as if they were hopeless.

"Practice is over! I'll see you all at the game tomorrow, twelve o'clock sharp!"

He turned and looked right at George and the serious look was back. "And remember. *No dogs allowed!*"

Chet walked off the field.

The fun was gone from the game of Keep Away. Even Lucky seemed to know that the game was over. He dropped the ball and lay down in the grass.

One by one the Expos came by and gave Lucky a pat on the head as they headed home. It would be Lucky's last practice with them.

Finally only Lucky and George were left on the field. George sat down in the bleachers.

Coach Chet was serious about baseball. He knew a lot about baseball. He had helped George a lot with his batting today.

Maybe Chet was right. Maybe they *would* be better off without a dog on the team. Lucky had caused a lot of trouble at the practice, just as Coach Chet said he would. George looked at Lucky sniffing under the bleachers.

And what about the tobacco? George felt the bulge in his back pocket.

"You can't play baseball without chewing tobacco."

Was Chet right about that too?

George pulled the envelope out of his back

pocket and looked at it. He smoothed out the package and read the label. "The South's finest chew," it said.

Then in tiny letters at the bottom it said, "Warning: This product may cause mouth cancer."

Chet wouldn't give them anything that would hurt them, would he?

George stared for a few minutes at the bag. He thought about the brown liquid that Chet had been spitting out. It had looked disgusting.

But. . .

He wanted to be a good baseball player, like Chet. It wouldn't hurt to check it out.

The packet felt heavy in his hand.

He unrolled the top and looked inside at the brown stringy stuff.

He poked his nose down into the bag and sniffed. The tobacco didn't smell too bad this time. It smelled like an old pipe of his grandfather's that his mother had kept.

He wondered what it would feel like. It wouldn't hurt to feel it. He took out a small pinch of the tobacco and rolled it around in his hand. It felt damp and warm.

He wondered what it would be like to taste it. Chet did it. Surely it wouldn't hurt him to take a little taste.

He looked at the tobacco in his hand for a long time.

Then he put it into his mouth and began to chew.

Dog Heaven

Lucky was sniffing around under the bleachers. It was a gold mine of dog goodies.

To his right was half a box of popcorn scattered in a pile. Someone had been kind enough to spill a Coke on top of it.

Dog heaven!

To his left was half of a hot dog. He carefully ate the hot dog out of the bun and left the bread. It had mustard on it.

Delicious!

He sniffed at a piece of chewed bubble gum but decided to pass on it.

He looked up through the bleachers at the boy. He was sitting on the bottom row of

seats, eating something out of an envelope.

Great! The boy always shared with him.

Lucky hurried over to the boy and quickly sat up on his hind legs. He had taught the boy to give him goodies when he sat on his hind legs.

The boy always had the best things to eat. Sometimes he gave Lucky bites of hamburger and sometimes bites of cheese. Once he had even given Lucky a whole ice-cream cone.

George had held the cone for him while he licked out every bit of the soft ice cream. Just remembering that cone made his mouth water. The boy always had the best goodies!

He waited now, in begging position, for the boy to share.

"No, boy!" said the boy.

No?

Lucky would have to try harder. He tried his cutest look. A look that would soften any

heart. A look that his mother had taught him especially for times like this.

"No!" the boy said again.

Lucky tried one more time.

His Demand Bark would surely work.

"ERF!"

"No, Lucky," said the boy and he got up to leave.

Lucky watched the boy walk away. He was still up on his hind legs. He was still giving the boy his best look.

He couldn't believe his bad luck.

Slowly he lowered himself from his begging position and began to follow the boy home. The boy was not going to share today.

He watched as the boy tucked the envelope into his jacket pocket. In his mind Lucky marked the spot. He never forgot where goodies were hidden. If the boy had eaten some of whatever was in the envelope then sometime, somehow, Lucky would try it too.

All the way home he kept his eyes on the

pocket. All the way into the house and up the stairs, he watched and waited.

He was sure he would have his chance later.

The boy lay down on his bed. He didn't look well. He looked sick. Lucky jumped up on the bed and poked his nose in the boy's face. He licked him a few times but the boy did not pay any attention to him.

Suddenly the boy sat up straight. He jumped off the bed and ran down the hall to the bathroom. Lucky tilted his head and barked at the boy.

Something was wrong.

Lucky lay back down on the bed to wait for the boy to come back.

The day had started out to be another wonderful summer day. What had gone wrong? In only one day he had gone from the highest life a dog could possibly have to the lowest.

Lucky stretched out, his head toward the pillow.

He stopped. He realized that he was lying on the jacket. *The* jacket. The jacket that had the boy's envelope in it.

Lucky glanced at the door. No sign of the boy. He began to sniff in the jacket for the envelope. When he found the pocket he tried to push into it with his nose. He could not reach the envelope. As he pushed, the jacket fell down onto the floor.

The envelope fell out.

He had it!

A strong smell came from the envelope. Could this really be it?

Without wasting a second Lucky pawed at the rolled end of the envelope and it opened.

He could hear the boy coming down the hall. He had to hurry. The stuff inside didn't smell good but he was out of time.

He gulped down three bites. Then he ran downstairs and out into the backyard.

Success!

Moans and Groans

George lay down on his bed and moaned.
Ooooo!

Pains were hitting his stomach in waves. When he closed his eyes, he was swept away by dizziness.

He reached out and tried to put one foot on the floor to steady himself, but it didn't help.

Oooooo!

He groaned again. His hands trembled.

This made you a better ball player?

It made no sense to George. This stuff only made him sick.

He rested his head on the pillow. Another wave hit him.

He sat up. He was going to be sick again. He stood up and ran for the bathroom.

In the bathroom he sat down on the side of the tub and put his head on his knees. What was he going to do?

He looked up at the medicine cabinet. He remembered that his mother always gave him pink medicine for an upset stomach. This was the worst upset stomach he had ever had.

With the last of his strength he wobbled down the hall to the top of the steps and called his mother.

"Mom."

"Yes, George," she answered from the kitchen where she was cooking dinner. A smell of onions came up from the kitchen.

The smell made George feel dizzy again.

"Mom, I have an upset stomach. Can I take a spoonful of the pink medicine?" he asked.

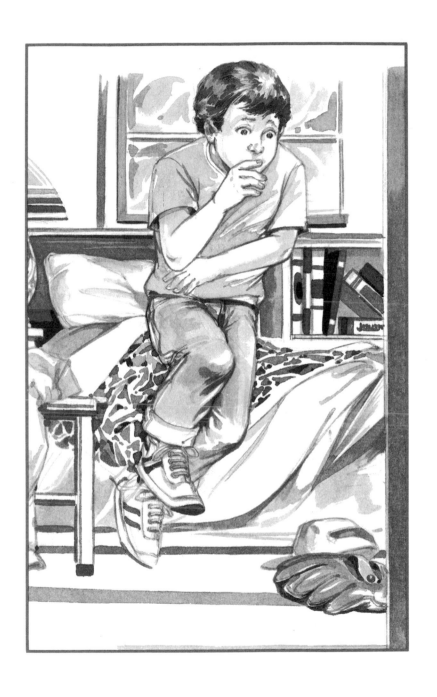

His mother hurried up the stairs.

"You're white as a sheet!" she said. "Come on in the bathroom. Have you been eating junk food at the ball park again?"

George didn't answer.

He followed her down the hall. He watched as she opened the mirrored door and took down the bottle of pink medicine. She picked up the medicine spoon and measured out his dose.

He hoped it would work.

"Go on to bed, honey," she said. "You don't look like you want to eat tonight."

George thought about the onion smell and nodded.

Slowly, like an eighty-year-old man, he headed back to his room.

Slowly, like an eighty-year-old man, he lowered himself gently onto the bed. He hoped the bed would not spin around this time.

Slowly, like an eighty-year-old man, he closed his eyes.

Why had Chet given him the tobacco? Life just got a little more complicated. Chet was wrong.

Tomorrow he would give the package back. Tomorrow he might be off the team. Chet was in charge of the team now. But George still was in charge of himself.

He closed his eyes again.

He thought about Lucky locked in the storage shed. Lucky trusted him. He had let Lucky down today.

He thought about Lucky wanting the tobacco. He remembered Lucky sitting up begging for a bite.

He was thankful for one thing—he had not given Lucky any of the tobacco. If Lucky had taken a bite of the tobacco, he would be sick too.

George was sick enough. He was sure a little dog would not be able to survive this.

A new wave of dizziness swept over him but this time it swept him into sleep.

More
Moans and Groans

Lucky lay in the tall grass behind the ball field. He didn't feel like moving at all. His stomach hurt and every time he tried to stand up, he felt dizzy.

He had run from the house at top speed. He had hidden in the tall grass behind center field, past the white fence. He had been afraid that the boy would be angry about the envelope.

He couldn't worry about that. He could only think about the terrible feeling in his stomach.

Lucky tried to get up again. He put one leg out and straightened it. He fell back like a

newborn puppy trying to walk. He couldn't get his balance.

He sank back into the tall cool grass.

He felt miserable. If he had had the energy, he would have given the Misery Howl but today a Misery Moan would have to do.

Oooo!

A deep moan came from his throat. It was low and soft. No one could hear him now. No one could help him now.

Oooooo!

For the first time since he had come to live with the boy, he wanted his mother. He wished with all his heart that she was with him now.

He closed his eyes and remembered the wonderful warm feeling of snuggling against his mother with his brother and sister—a warm ball of puppies. He had felt so safe.

Oooooo!

He tried to remember what his mother

would do. His mother had taught him what to do for an upset stomach.

Eat grass.

Grass was a dog's best medicine.

He leaned over and tried to get a mouthful of grass but he was too weak. If only he could reach the cool green grass, he knew he would feel better.

He rolled his eyes around to look at the green grass. He nipped a little at one of the blades of grass, then another and another until his strength was gone.

He closed his eyes and rested his head down on the grass.

He had done everything that he could. He still felt terrible.

He could think only of the pain in his stomach as he slipped into sleep.

No Lucky

George woke up feeling that something was wrong. Something was different this morning.

He reached up and rubbed his head. He had a headache but that was not it.

His mouth felt dry and tasted terrible but that was not it.

His stomach rumbled but that was not it.

He remembered the chewing tobacco and the terrible feeling of it settled on him.

He felt a lot better today. But . . .

What was wrong?

No Lucky.

That was what was wrong. Every morning

since he had had Lucky, Lucky had come upstairs to wake him up.

Lucky would run upstairs and jump on the bed. He would dig at the covers until he could see George's face. Then he would lick and lick and lick until George would start to laugh. They would roll around and wrestle on the bed.

Today there was no licking and laughing and wrestling.

Lucky wasn't there.

George got up and began to get dressed.

He thought back to the day before. He really couldn't blame Lucky for being mad at him. He had locked him in the storage shed at the ball park. He had not let Lucky play baseball.

The thought of Lucky sitting up on his back legs begging for the tobacco made his throat tight. Lucky could not have known why George did not share with him.

George looked at the clock. It was almost

ten o'clock. Lucky usually got him up at 7:05.

He had slept all morning. He had a ball game in two hours.

He quickly pulled on his jeans and T-shirt. Today would be his last baseball game. Today he would give back the tobacco.

It had caused him enough trouble.

First, though, he had to find Lucky.

He reached down and picked up his jacket from the floor. Then he stopped and stared.

On the floor back under the bed was the red-and-white envelope. The end was unrolled. Some of the tobacco was scattered around.

Lucky!

Lucky had eaten some of the tobacco!

George sat down on the edge of the bed. He knew why Lucky was gone. Lucky was sick.

George could see claw marks where Lucky had clawed the end of the packet open.

How much had Lucky eaten? There was no way to tell.

He had to find Lucky. Wherever Lucky was, he was sick. He needed George.

He had to find him . . . soon.

He stuffed the packet into his back pocket. He ran downstairs to the kitchen and looked in front of the refrigerator where Lucky always slept.

No Lucky.

He ran into the backyard to the doghouse.

No Lucky.

He ran around to the front of the house and began to call Lucky.

"Here, Lucky. Here, boy."

His voice sounded desperate.

He *was* desperate.

George had been very sick the night before, but he had had medicine to make him better. Lucky had nothing. Lucky was in trouble and it was George's fault.

He ran back into the kitchen and left a note for his mother: GONE TO FIND LUCKY.

He hurried down the street. Jill and Kritter were throwing the baseball back and forth in Jill's yard.

"Lucky is gone!" George called out to them. "Lucky may be sick. I've got to find him!"

Jill dropped the baseball. Kritter dropped his glove. They began to run with George.

"Here, Lucky. Here, boy!"

One by one all the kids on the team joined the search.

They split up and covered the neighborhood street by street. They checked all of Lucky's favorite places.

The backyard where he always chased the tabby cat. The frozen yogurt stand. Ms. Haines's backyard where Lucky liked to dig around her Japanese dogwoods. Under the bleachers at the ball field. Ms. Watts's back door where she always left a dish of cat food.

The kids met in front of George's house.

One by one they ran back with the bad news.

No Lucky.

No Lucky.

No Lucky.

They had been looking for nearly two hours. They all sank down exhausted on the grass.

Kritter looked down at his watch. "It's twelve o'clock," he said. "Time for our game."

"Go on," said George. "I can't play without Lucky."

The Expos didn't move. They looked down at the grass.

Kritter jumped up. "Come on," he said. "Lucky loves ball games. He has never missed a ball game. Maybe Lucky will come when he hears us playing."

George struggled up to his feet.

He didn't know where else to look.

If he couldn't find Lucky, maybe Lucky could find him.

George headed for the ball field. He hoped that Kritter was right.

Dog Dreams

Lucky lay in the tall green grass behind the ball field, hidden from view. He was in a deep sleep.

He had had many dog dreams before. Usually they were wonderful.

Once he dreamed he was chasing the tabby cat. In his dream he wasn't in the backyard. He was in a jungle, full of vines and wild jungle smells. He chased the tabby cat over rocks and through overgrown paths. He cornered him in a dark cave. No means of escape. Then he woke up.

Another time, lying in the backseat of the station wagon, he dreamed of every food he

had ever eaten. There was roast beef, thick slices of cheddar cheese, beef jerky strips, ice cream, hot dogs, and best of all, HAM. His mouth had been watering when he woke up.

As he lay in the grass, his dreams were not good. Lucky was having his worst nightmare ever.

He dreamed he was back at the old house where he had lived under the steps with his mother before they were taken to the pound. The man from the pound was chasing him around the yard with a big noose on the end of a stick. Then he was at the ball field and the man was chasing him around the bases, round and round.

Lucky kept barking for George to come and rescue him but George would not come. In the dream he could see George with another dog. George was playing ball with the other dog.

Lucky whimpered in his sleep. His feet walked back and forth in the air.

In his dream he could hear the sounds of baseball.

The cheers of the teams, the crack of the bat, the thud of the ball hitting the ground in the outfield.

"Play ball!" he heard a voice call out.

He began to bark and kick in his sleep but he could not get out of the dream. Just when the noose began to slip over his head, his eyes snapped open. He woke up.

His heart was beating hard and fast from his nightmare.

He rolled over gently and lay still in the grass.

He was still a little weak but his stomach didn't hurt anymore.

His mother had been right! Grass did the trick. He tried out his legs and he could stand.

Where was he anyway?

He sniffed the ground. Popcorn, leather, sweat, boys and girls and . . . *his* boy!

He listened carefully.

Crack!

The baseball sounds in his dream had been real! There was a game going on right now and he was in the grass behind the field.

He began to move toward the sounds of the ball game. He could hear the kids, and the ball thumping down . . . into left field.

His left field.

The Expos were playing and they needed him. He had to get to left field. Lucky began to run.

He felt good and strong now. His sickness was over and George was near.

Feeling well, a sunny day, a baseball game, and his own boy. This was better than any dog dream that he could imagine.

One Hundred
Dog Licks

George stood on third base. The game was almost over and still Lucky had not come. George wasn't interested in the game. He kept thinking about Lucky.

George felt his back pocket again. The packet of chewing tobacco was still there. Lucky had seen him take a bite. Lucky had thought it was good because George had taken some.

George had let Lucky down. George looked down at the ground. His vision blurred.

Crack!

The batter hit a grounder right to George.

George let it roll on by. He didn't feel like a baseball player anymore.

The ball rolled into left field. No one was there to get it. It rolled on into the tall grass.

Chet ran up the third base line, yelling *"Get it! Get it!"* His face was red and he was excited.

Kritter ran to find it. The runner rounded second.

Chet came up to George and yelled, "What's the matter with you? You don't wanna play baseball?"

George looked at Coach Chet. Coach Chet was right about some things, but he was not right about everything. Coach Chet had let George down.

George reached back and pulled out the packet. He held it out to Chet.

"I don't want this," he said. "This stuff's not good for you. It made me sick last night."

Chet's face was red. He took the packet from George. He wasn't yelling now.

The runner rounded third but George

didn't care. He turned and began to walk off the field. He would be off the team now for sure.

The other kids watched silently.

Chet took off his hat and scratched his head. He watched George walk away.

The batter slowed as he ran toward home. No one was trying to get him out.

"Hey," Chet turned to the other kids. "You wanna play baseball?"

The Expos looked back at him. No one said "Yes."

Everyone watched George.

From somewhere close by they heard a bark.

ERF!

Again.

ERF! ERF!

George began to run toward the bark. A small streak appeared out of the tall grass. A streak of moving legs and flapping ears. A small dog with a ball in his mouth.

Lucky!

A cheer rose up from the Expos. George ran hard toward Lucky. The Expos followed.

Somewhere in left field they met. George held out his arms. Lucky made a giant leap. Down they went onto the field. Lucky gave George about one hundred dog licks.

The Expos caught up with them. There was a giant pile of kids on the ball field, patting Lucky and cheering.

Chet stood for a second watching the pile of kids. He frowned his serious frown. Then he shook his head, and waved his glove in the "you are hopeless" wave. He walked off the field.

The runner continued on toward home.

George held Lucky and patted him over and over. Everything was all right now. Lucky was back. Lucky was well.

The runner trotted slowly across home base.

George hugged Lucky one more big hug as in the distance the umpire called:

"SAFE!"

Way to Go!

Coach Chet walked over to the trash can at the side of the ball field. He threw the package of tobacco away. Then he walked back and faced the players. He had his serious baseball frown on his face.

"One thing about good baseball," he said, "is keeping an open mind. You can't be a good ball player if you can't learn new things."

He looked down at the ground and kicked a small stone.

"Here's the deal. If the mutt behaves himself and continues to field those grounders like he did just now, he stays. I'm going to try

hard and you're going to try harder." He looked right at George. "No one chews tobacco on my team," he said. "Now. You wanna play baseball?"

"Yes!" yelled George.

"Yes!" yelled Kritter and Jay and Jill and the rest of the Expos.

Chet looked back at George holding Lucky. "Does *he* want to play baseball?" He pointed to Lucky.

"Yes!" said all the Expos together.

Chet shook his head.

"Play ball!" he said.

The team took their positions. The Expos were ready. George on third. Mike on first. Kritter on second. Jill at short stop. Jay pitching. Steve catching. Right field, Millie. Center field, Tripp. And in left field, Lucky.

ERF! ERF!

The game continued.

A kid named Tom came up to bat for the Braves. Jay threw the ball.

Tom connected. The ball flew straight up.

Jill stepped back. She got under the ball. The ball dropped slowly down to her. She made a pocket, and *plop*, the ball fell right into her mitt. She trapped the ball with her other hand.

"Out!" called the umpire.

"Way to go!" yelled Chet.

Jay wound up again.

Another Brave came up to bat.

Jay looked at Chet. Chet nodded. One by one the Expos nodded to each other. The play was at first.

Jay threw the ball.

Crack! A grounder.

The ball rolled straight to Jay. He scooped it up and, like a machine, threw the ball to Mike at first.

"OUT!" the umpire called.

"Way to go!" Chet yelled.

All the Expos yelled. One more out and they would win the game. One more out and the ten-game losing streak would be over.

ERF! ERF!

Lucky was ready.

Coach Chet gave the nod again. The play was at first.

Jay wound up and threw to the kid at bat.

Crack!

The ball hit the bat with a solid whack. The kind of whack that meant the ball was history.

The batter put down the bat slowly and began to walk toward first. He didn't hurry. He was sure it was an automatic home run.

The ball flew over the tall grass toward the white fence. It was too far gone. None of the Expos ran for it. None, that is, except a small streak of moving legs and flapping ears. The ball fell just inside the white fence. Lucky grabbed the ball and headed for George.

Lucky burst out of the tall grass with the ball in his mouth. The runner saw Lucky with the ball and began to hurry.

"Come on, Lucky!" George yelled.

Lucky slid into George. George took the

ball from Lucky's mouth and threw it hard and fast toward first.

There was one second of silence. The ball soared toward first. The runner began to slide. Mike reached out his glove. *Smack!* The ball hit.

"OUT!"

A cheer arose from the Expos. The ten-game losing streak was over. They had won the game!

"Way to go!" yelled Chet. The Expos jumped up and down and yelled. Chet threw his glove into the air and jumped up and down with them.

George picked Lucky up onto his shoulder and held him high. The team began a cheer.

"Lucky! Lucky! Lucky!"

The Expos carried Lucky across the field in a victory march.

Chet shook his head and laughed at Lucky. The serious baseball look was gone.

"Okay," he said. "The mutt's on the team!"

The Expos cheered again.

George lowered Lucky from his shoulder and gave him a hug. "We're going to be great!" he said.

Lucky barked twice. It was his favorite: The Happiness Bark.

About the author

Betsy Duffey was born in Anderson, South Carolina, and is a graduate of Clemson University. She is the author of *The Math Wiz*, *The Gadget War*, and *A Boy in the Doghouse*. The character, Lucky, was inspired by her puppy, Chester, and the ten other dogs her family has owned over the years.

Betsy Duffey lives with her husband and two sons in Atlanta, Georgia.

About the illustrator

Leslie Morrill has illustrated many books for children, including *A Boy in the Doghouse*. He lives in Chevy Chase, Maryland.

'How it works'

THE
SISTER

by J.A. HAZELEY, N.S.F.W.
and J.P. MORRIS, O.M.G.

(Authors of 'And Then
There Were Nuns')

A LADYBIRD BOOK FOR GROWN-UPS

This is a sister.

Wherever you go, whatever you do, a sister will always be there.

Which can get really annoying.

It is the five minutes of the month when Anthony is not annoying his sister, Annabel.

The rest of the time he calls her "Annasmell," hides her school-bag, flicks at her chicken pox scars and occasionally tortures her teddy–bear with a fork.

"They play so nicely together, don't they?" say their parents.

Sisters like to have fun with their brothers.

"Let's jump over that hedge," says Zara to her little brother.

"Yes, let's!" he says.

"You go first," says Zara.

These two sisters are very different.

Megan, the red−haired one, likes running across the fields and whinnying. Lara, the lighter−coloured one, likes eating whole apples and bales of hay.

Their horses are also sisters.

In a big family, brothers and sisters will often inherit a lot of hand—me—down clothes.

When Coleen grows out of her brother Thomas's old jumper, she will hand it on to her little sister Bridget.

Bridget's wardrobe is so out of fashion she might as well go to school in a doublet and a ruff.

Because he spent all morning spoiling her marble run, Eva is making her big brother Barney sit through Thumberella 3: Flight To The Marshmallow Rainbow.

Eva does not really want to watch the film. But she does really want to watch Barney fuming.

Barney will spend the next six weeks singing the big song from the film at her.

Eva cannot win.

"I don't know why you can't be nice to your little brother," says Maggie's mum.

"We all have to get along in this family."

Maggie has never met her Uncle Pete because her mum pretends he lives in New Zealand.

"Tell them it was your idea to dry my shoes in the toaster," says Corinna.

Poor little Grover starts crying.

He can't even reach the toaster.

Emily and her brother Alfie have invented a joke that makes them laugh until they hurt, but which nobody else understands. They are saying it again and again.

Mum and Dad would like to have a word with whoever it was who said that nothing is better than the sound of children's laughter.

Kerry is Zach's sister.

She will always be there for her brother, throughout their lives, because that is what a sister does.

He will be there for his sister until he becomes a teenager. Then he will only be there when he would like to be introduced to one of her friends or get some advice about how girls work.

Because that is what a brother does.

"Are you asleep yet?" Maisie asks her older brother for the forty–eighth time since they went to bed three hours ago.

He is not, and it is now midnight.

He is woken by his little sister just before five o'clock the next morning. She has thought of a new question.

"Are you awake yet?"

Lottie and Morgan share so many memories of growing up together. Now they are older, they often talk about all the things they did.

"Did not," says Lottie.

"Did," says Morgan.

"Did not," says Lottie.

"Did," says Morgan.

"Did not," says Lottie.

Corrie is another sort of sister. She is a nursing sister in a hospital ward.

There are no nursing brothers in hospitals, because patients take longer to get better when they are always expecting a wedgie or a Nerf-gun bullet in the ear.

Since she last had a haircut, Leonie has been promoted, got married, moved into a new home and had the all—clear from the hospital. She has plenty to tell Suzanne the hairdresser.

"How's your brother?" Suzanne asks as Leonie sits down.

Leonie's brother is the bass player in Liam Gallagher's new band.

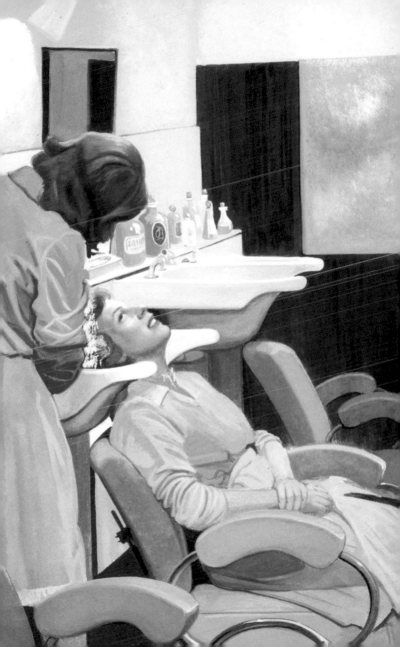

Ralf is on the telephone to his solicitor.

"And you're absolutely sure there's no such thing as a sibling divorce?" he asks.

Poor Ralf.

Nemesis is one of three sisters. She was never sporty, but her sisters Venus and Serena have done rather well for themselves.

"I am very happy for them," says Nemesis, when people ask. "But I do not really think about them much."

Teaching keeps Nemesis nice and busy. And there is always lots to do at the League Against Tennis.

Hjørdis always used to fight with Agnek about whose turn it was to sleep on the top bunk.

"You're the oldest. Draw up a rota," their mum told Hjørdis.

Agnek is old enough to read now. She notices that her time for the top bunk seems to be while she is at school, not while she is asleep.

The rota says they will be swapping just in time for Hjørdis to go to college.

Bernadette says she wants to be the "Bad Auntie" for her sister's daughter Alice.

"I'll introduce her to drinking and swearing and all the fun, bad stuff," promises Bernadette.

Bernadette has bought little Alice a six-pound pat of butter as a Christening present.

"Start as I mean to go on," burps Bernadette.

Over the years, Gareth has bought his sister Kelly every possible birthday present he can find related to a film he remembers her enjoying in 1989.

Kelly has had to come to terms with the idea that though they spent half of their lives together, Gareth was not really paying attention for most of it.

Siona is a teacher. Her brother Lachlan is a senior partner in a legal firm.

For their mum and dad's wedding anniversary, Siona carved them a personalised "Ron and Maria" key rack for the hall.

Lachlan, who remembered the anniversary at the last minute, got his P.A. to order them a boat.

"Lachlan, you shouldn't have," says his mum.

Samantha and Leonard are twins.

"Not identical, of course!" Samantha always explains.

Leonard thinks that is rubbing it in a bit.

Broderick and his sister Bemily used to spend time together because they were children and had nowhere else to live.

Now they have their own houses, they spend time together because it reminds them of the time they used to spend time together.

Talking about the time they used to spend together is almost interesting enough to pass the time they now spend together.

Marianne and Clive have been arguing for two days about what to do with Mum's bungalow.

Marianne has agreed to put the argument behind her for the duration of their trapeze act.

She hopes Clive has done the same.

"Did not," says Lottie.

"Did," says Morgan.

"Did not," says Lottie.

"Did," says Morgan.

"Did not," says Lottie.

THE AUTHORS would like to record their gratitude and offer their apologies to the many Ladybird artists whose luminous work formed the glorious wallpaper of countless childhoods. Revisiting it for this book as grown-ups has been a privilege.

MICHAEL JOSEPH

UK | USA | Canada | Ireland | Australia
India | New Zealand | South Africa

Michael Joseph is part of the Penguin Random House group of companies
whose addresses can be found at global.penguinrandomhouse.com

First published 2017
002

Copyright © Jason Hazeley and Joel Morris, 2017
All images copyright © Ladybird Books Ltd, 2017

The moral right of the authors has been asserted

Printed in Italy by L.E.G.O. S.p.A

A CIP catalogue record for this book is available from the British Library

ISBN: 978–0–718–18870–2

www.greenpenguin.co.uk

Penguin Random House is committed to a sustainable future for our business, our readers and our planet. This book is made from Forest Stewardship Council® certified paper.